THE WOLF'S SECRET
VEGAS BRIDE

A HOWLS Romance

EVE LANGLAIS

DANITA LEARNED HOW TO ESCAPE BY WATCHING movies. It made for fascinating study, the many ways a bolt for freedom could go wrong. She took mental notes on how to accomplish the feat. Only an idiot would write anything down. She left nothing *he* could find.

A prisoner to his whims, she smiled and pretended while she plotted her breakout. She couldn't afford to make a mistake. Any kind of misstep and he'd find her.

He always found her because she lacked the kind of courage needed to put a permanent end to his reign of terror. One day maybe he'd push her far enough and she'd do the unthinkable.

Do I have the strength to deliver the killing blow?

Best to just flee instead of finding out.

It was the movie *Sleeping with the Enemy* that gave her an idea of how to accomplish her grand exit. Except Danita was smart and learned from that heroine's mistake. She didn't flush the ring—that heavy monstrosity that was meant to signify she belonged to him. Dani—which she preferred over the more formal Danita—tossed the symbol of her oppression into the lake while she kayaked.

Plop. The metal band barely made a noise or ripple as it hit the water and sank. No one saw her toss it because, not only had she paddled far enough out from the remote cabin, a light mist on the water, the kind fall mornings were famous for, shrouded her.

The water she stroked through appeared dark, cold, and unforgiving. Scary, too. What lurked in the depths? She'd seen some of the fish pulled from it. Large, with big mouths that flexed, filled with rows of tiny teeth. Everyone claimed they didn't bite people. She wondered if those they bit simply never lived to tell.

That thought plagued her as she drew close to the second part of the plan, which involved entering the water. Perhaps she should find another route of escape.

She peered back over her shoulder. The cabin—momentarily appearing, a hazy shape in the white fog—her prison. A reminder of what awaited if she chickened out.

Suck it up, buttercup. It was what her dad used to say.

But he was gone. *Just me, myself, and I.*

"Danita, where are you?"

The voice, deep and hard, echoed over the water, sounding closer than it was. A strange feature of most still bodies of water. The way sound traveled could play tricks on the mind.

She knew *he* was on shore. But he could have been in arm's reach, given how his voice curled around her.

What is he doing at the cabin already? He was not supposed to have started looking yet.

I'll have to abort. Only she didn't want to. She couldn't go back.

Wouldn't.

"Danita?" A terse note entered his voice. A note that meant he was about to lose his temper. Her cheek throbbed, a hint of a bruise still yellowing the skin.

"Are you out here?" The query held a note of doubt. He remained unsure where she was. She'd done the job of hiding her tracks well. Inside the house, she had kept the windows closed as she ran a self-clean on the oven, filling the place with an acrid stench of burning debris. Outside, the geraniums she'd asked for and gotten, perfumed the air, further masking her scent.

Would it be enough?

She held her breath, wondering if he'd guess she'd gone for a row. He shouldn't. The kayaks were put away for the season. She'd had to sneak one down to the shore from the shed.

"Danita, if you're out here, you'd better not be hiding. Answer me!" His voice lost volume as he moved away, seeking her. It wouldn't be the first time he searched. She'd developed a naughty habit of disappearing but remaining nearby.

She'd been conditioning him the past few weeks. Purposely not answering. Sometimes even moving room to room ahead of him to avoid detection. Making sure he found her before he completely snapped. Then she'd casually stroll in to wherever he was, wearing earphones each time. Classical music he discovered when he ripped the buds from her ears. Each time she'd smiled falsely and said, "I'm sorry, were you calling for me? I didn't hear you." She did this over and over. Each time his search effort took a little longer. The last time he'd given up for over an hour before truly setting out to find her.

A door slammed. He'd gone inside. It was time. She placed the oar on the kayak and slipped into the water, the buoyant life vest she wore old, but serviceable. The one she usually used would be found, stashed on the kayak, because sometimes she preferred the ease of movement. He let her kayak on sunny days while he watched so he knew her habits.

She held tight to the waterproof satchel she'd been preparing the past few weeks. Hidden behind the toilet paper and tampons in her bathroom. It held the money she'd squirreled away. More than expected since she'd found a secret stash of bills inside a hollowed book. It lacked the crispness of new money, but at least it was still usable. Inside the bag, a change of clothes. She didn't dare bring much since her plan hinged on him thinking she drowned.

If he thinks I'm dead, then he won't come after me. She'd be free.

He'll find me.

The pessimism whispered. The fear of failure made her shiver in the chill water. Her stroke remained steady.

She had to stick to the plan. Make it appear as an

accident. The lake was deep, and farther down, there was a current that fed a small river that rapidly grew rough. The rapids passed through some rocky terrain and then an abrupt waterfall that pooled into a basin that would make any search attempt difficult.

But he will still go looking. He had plans for her. Plans she kept denying. Her one saving grace? His ego demanded that she beg him to sleep with her. It would never happen. But he refused to believe her when she said, "Never in a million years."

"You'll want me." His confident reply.

Want a man that made her stomach clench in fear? Who repulsed her on every level?

She stroked faster through the water. No amount of threat by him would ever make her that desperate.

She kept angling, feeling the weight of the satchel dragging at her. The vest helped, letting her float, but she'd not counted on how quickly her arms would feel leaden. The chill water sapped at her strength.

Perhaps she should have kept the kayak and ridden it all the way to the other side of the lake. Too late to change her mind now. Tense with fear, she sluiced through the water, listening intently for sound, ignoring the dark morass below her, certain her harsh breaths of exertion and panic carried across the water.

How long before he realized she was well and truly gone?

She heard no more yelling, but there was no mistaking the sudden roar of a motor.

Was he leaving? The luck would be incredible. It

might be hours before he returned and knew she'd slipped her leash.

She sliced through the water, hoping she moved in the right direction. The waterproof compass she'd sewn to the satchel pointed for her. She swam for days. At least it seemed forever in the timeless mist.

And she'd obviously missed her direction because the gentle tug of a current took her by surprise. She kicked harder, working away from it, and eventually hit the shore on the northwest side. She was probably two miles from the house. Not far enough.

The shoreline proved rocky, and her water shoes did little to protect her from the bite. The chill air pimpled what was exposed of her skin. She didn't dare take a moment to strip. She needed to move fast. Except wouldn't she do that better not laden down by a heavy bag?

It pulled against her upper body, what seemed like little supplies a heavy weight. The shivering and chattering teeth decided her.

This would be for naught if she died of hypothermia or because she got tired too quick.

She stripped off her wetsuit before rolling it into a tight ball. She held it and looked around. Stuffing it in her satchel was unnecessary weight.

That suit is your ring. The one thing that doesn't flush. She knew that, and yet weighing her options, she chose to shove it in the crevice of a downed tree trunk. Hopefully it would be shredded by animals and the weather before it was found.

The important part was escaping. The longer *he* thought her drowned the better. If Dani could just break free...then it wouldn't matter. She grabbed the track suit from her bag, pulling on the thicker fleece with relief. The water shoes she swapped for her runners. Old ones she used for gardening and usually kept stored in the shed. She tucked her water shoes with the wetsuit in the trunk. Dead leaves shoved over them added more camouflage.

Sucking in a deep breath—*Holy crap, I am really doing this*—she set off. There was no trail to follow, just a memorized map of the area and a compass with condensation inside its glass face. She followed the bobbing needle northwest, hoping her navigational skills were up to par. In the city, she'd never had to learn more than the transit route. There were signs and people to ask if she was uncertain of her location. Out here in the wilderness, she was alone—and hunted.

How she missed the city with its hustle and bustle and the people all around. People meant safety. How long since she'd talked to anyone other than *him* and his loyal crew?

The mist persisted on land. It hung even thicker than on the water in some spots. It curled around the trees, giving them strange shapes, the gray tendrils living smoky limbs.

The worse part, though? The panic. She kept imagining movement, causing more than one mini heart attack. *Is that someone standing over there?* Her head would sharply turn to peek. Her breath hitched before gushing out in relief at the false alarm. Thus far, it was just the mist swirling and teasing the shadows. Mocking her fear.

Some people feared an imaginary bogeyman. Dani actually had a real one. He was a monster. And the one thing about monsters was they didn't like to be thwarted.

Given she couldn't rely on her eyes, she didn't know the land, and there were no convenient signs, she consulted her compass often, hoping she was getting close.

This area of the Muskokas didn't have dense habitation because it served as a playground for those who liked to have acres between them and their neighbors. But what it lacked for in population, it made up for in toys. As in garages and sheds full of mechanical vehicles. Like the ATVs and dirt bikes *he* had complained about, ripping through the woods. Boy toys that would prove her salvation.

It took more time than she liked, the hike from water to her destination. She'd landed a little too early and had to pivot at one point when a sharp upturn in the land required skirting. But that turned out to be a good thing. She found a clearing where someone had chopped down some trees and begun removing them. The trail of crushed underbrush, and the occasional rut in the dirt from wheels, gave her a direction to follow. A clear path didn't erase her fear. With the number of times her heart stopped, she was pretty sure she'd shaved a decade off her life. Her first genuine sigh of relief didn't happen until she discerned the denser shape of the house in the swirling mist.

She'd found it. A small victory. Now the question was—anybody home?

The spacious yard around it made her feel exposed as she dashed across, the open pockets she could see moving constantly with the fog. Would someone lunge from the mist?

She heard no voice, naught but the frantic heave of her breaths.

The patio had three steps, and she raced up them, heading for the sliding glass door. She faced it, seeing a wild-eyed version of herself. Her blonde hair wisped in curls around her face where it had escaped from her bun. She slapped the door, the sound sharp in the quiet morning.

She paused, listening.

A gut instinct said the house was vacant.

You're all alone out here.

She wanted to be wrong. Let someone be inside. Surely, they'd help her.

No one came to the sliding door for a glance outside.

She wasn't truly surprised. *He*'d been cautious, only bringing her in late fall. A dead season for most folks. Those living in this playhouse for the rich—the thick, fat beams perfectly interlocked on this custom log home— only came during the summer and deep winter. No one wanted chilly, damp autumn, especially in the middle of the week.

Since the sliding glass door wouldn't budge, the security bar firmly wedged, she skipped down off the porch and skirted around the house. Dani passed by the shed—and all its lovely engines—in favor of the front of the house. This was the part of the plan fraught with possible problems. It hinged on her getting into the house fairly easily.

The good news was they didn't have an alarm system. *He* bitched about it all the time, that they were too remote for him to put something decent in place. A good thing or she would have had to learn to disarm it.

The knob didn't yield when she gripped it. No surprise given the driveway was empty of vehicles. She peeked around the area in front of the door, noting the lack of adornment except for a single planter tucked tight to the wall. It proved easy to tip, and she smiled as she spotted the single key under it.

The click of the turning tumblers seemed gunshot-loud in the stillness. She froze, not daring to breathe or move as she waited to see if someone would suddenly appear. She could almost hear the scary music playing as she remembered every single horror movie she'd seen about girls in the woods with fog. It didn't end well for them.

Nothing happened. For which her bladder said "thank you." Her panties remained dry as she entered the house.

I'm a criminal now. Breaking and entering. For a good reason, but still a taboo. *But you know what they say about the forbidden. It seduces. There is something inher-*

ently adrenalizing and terrifying about entering someone's home uninvited.

As soon as she stepped in, she was assailed by the scent of moth balls, a cottage must for those unused months. Everything was quiet and still except for the steady ticking of a clock on the wall. Was it really only eight-forty in the morning? No wonder fog still shrouded the land.

She stepped farther into the home, too scared to admire the wide plank floors and the woodwork that comprised this massive log home. She was more interested in other things, such as keys. Had the owners left the keys to the toys accessible? Wandering into the kitchen, with its massive farm sink and huge butcher block island, she immediately noticed a rack on the wall. Dangling from it was the object of her search, neatly labeled.

Dani ran her fingers over the metal treasures. ATV or bike? She had her choice. She snared both sets plus the one labeled "garage." In no time she exited the house, entered the garage, and was eyeing the machines. The bike sat on a triangular stool balancing the weight. Nothing too aggressive. 250CCs, not exactly a super powerful machine, but enough to get her going. And no, it wasn't odd she knew this. Her daddy taught her to ride at a young age. He taught her lots of things other daddies didn't teach their daughters. He just never taught her to defend herself.

I'll always keep you safe, baby girl, he'd said.

In order for that to work, he had to be around.

However, Daddy hadn't come home from his last business trip. And she needed him. Maybe he would have helped her spot the psycho from a mile away.

She realized she'd been staring blankly at the machines. Wasting time. Stupid. *Stay on track.*

Dani studied her choices. Despite the fact the ATV was new and big—a shiny red beast with a rack to strap her satchel—she opted for the bike. ATVs, while fast, were more cumbersome, and she felt a need for speed. *I can't get away from here fast enough.*

She tightened the satchel across her chest before grabbing the handlebars of the bike. She'd have to be careful yanking it off.

A slight tug and it barely rocked on the stand. She'd need to give it more muscle. She took in a breath and heaved. The bike lurched toward her, the weight of the front tipping harder than expected. Her arms dropped, and she heard a screech of metal.

The front and back tire hit the ground with a solid thud along with the muffler. She stared at the cylinder on the floor. Uh-oh. So much for a quiet exit. It wouldn't matter, though. He was gone. There was no one to hear. Even if his crew did, what would they do? There was nothing on the property they could use to chase her. *He* didn't want to risk her escaping.

The key went into the ignition easily, but she didn't turn it yet. She straddled the bike and walked it out of the shed Flintstone style. Once she started it, she'd better be ready to move. At least this time she could follow the road. A road wreathed in a thick mist.

She took in a deep breath. The silence pressed on her. The bugs, birds, everything so quiet this morning. She wanted to think she would succeed. Look how far she'd made it this time. Just a little farther to go.

A shiver walked down her spine, shattering that fragile hope. *He'll find me. He always finds me.*

Two months of being a prisoner. Two months of attempts. None in the last two weeks. He truly thought by burying her in the wilderness he'd foil her.

He'd miscalculated her determination.

The first kick of the starter pedal produced nothing but a click. *Turn it on, idiot.* Sometimes the basics could elude. She set the key into the right position, pulled the choke, and gave it some gas as she drove her foot down again on the lever. A stutter. *Nuh-nuh-nuh. Sputter.*

She kicked it again; it barely coughed.

Check the tank, dummy. Sure enough, the bike only had fumes left. She headed back into the garage and found a red can. There wasn't much left to pour in the tank, but that didn't matter. She only needed to go far enough to find civilization.

This time when she kicked the clutch, the bike shuddered as it coughed to life, the sound ridiculously loud. *Pop, pop, pop.* Like mini gunshots firing off.

The noise couldn't be helped. She held on tight and tucked up her foot as she cranked the throttle. The bike tore off, and she held in a shriek. It had been a few years since she'd ridden, but like a pedal bike, you never forgot. She straightened the wobble, and soon the wind streamed through her hair and face. She'd not thought to grab a helmet.

She almost turned around. Daddy always said safety first. In this case, safety wasn't what she put on her head but in the freedom that beckoned. Going back was giving *him* a chance to get his hands on her again. She couldn't allow that to happen.

Bent low over the bars, she sped, knowing she only had to make it to the main road. The main road where there was a blessed gas station, traffic, and a way out of here.

The end of the driveway opened onto the country road that meandered a few kilometers before it turned onto the main one. She spun onto it a bit fast and slid. Her heart jumped into her throat and almost gagged her.

She regained her balance and kept speeding. The crossroads neared. Freedom teased.

Almost there. She started to smile.

A truck threw itself across the T-intersection, a big, black king cab that she knew all too well. She screamed and turned rather than hit him head-on. *He found me.* He'd not been fooled at all by her preparations. But all was not lost. The main road was still close by. If she could just reach it.

Her turn brought her onto lumpy terrain back into the woods, a bumpier prospect, and yes, she could actually make a more direct beeline to her destination. If she made it to other people, he couldn't touch her.

Even over the kapowing of the muffler, she heard a roar behind her. Something pissed off.

Almost there. Almost there.

She chanted it over and over until she emerged from the woods, the shallow ditch sending her soaring to land on the road with a thump. She spun the bike, her heart clenching for a second when its weight seemed determined to keep spinning. She controlled it and gunned the gas. The tire spat stone before gripping and tearing off. The fog was thinner now, meaning she saw the stop sign for the intersection. But she could also see the lights of the vehicle behind her.

Too close.

She didn't slow down for the turn. She threw herself in the road, again counting on momentum to swing the bike. Only the road already had traffic!

The oncoming car, a huge sedan with a square hood, screeched as it applied the brakes, the klaxon of its horn loud and indignant. She would have waved her thanks for it not hitting her, but she needed both hands to hold on tight as she sped off, freedom so close she could almost taste it.

First thing I'm doing is I'm finding myself a vanilla banana sundae with caramel on top.

She wasn't free yet. A glance over her shoulder showed the black pickup penned behind the sedan that had narrowly missed her. Traffic on the other side prevented him from passing.

She didn't have much time.

The big sign appeared first, looming overhead, the flashing neon announcing it was open. Next, she saw the parking lot and the gas pumps. She whipped into the lot and braked. She jumped off the bike and let it hit the ground. She wouldn't need it now. She'd made it. Into the store she dashed, wild-eyed, wild-haired, and breathing as if she'd run a marathon.

The young guy behind the counter who sported the latest in retro mullets and sideburns looked up from his cellphone.

"Help me," she exclaimed.

"What do you need?"

"Can you call the police?"

"What for?"

"I need help. Quick. We don't have much time. He'll be here any minute."

"You look familiar. You live around here?"

"Yes and no. I was being held prisoner. I escaped. You have to help me."

He wagged a finger at her. "I know who you are. You're the broad living in that big place on Lost Trail Road."

"Yes." Her brow furrowed. "How do you know that?" Because from the moment of her arrival, no one was allowed to see her.

"Why don't you grab a drink while I make a call."

"I don't need a drink."

"Suit yourself." He turned around and put his phone to his ear. "Yeah. She's here."

Her blood ran cold.

She took a step back. Then another.

The mullet kid whirled back, and for a second, she hoped she was wrong, but then it happened. The same thing that happened to him. *Kelso*. The face elongated into a muzzle. The skin turned hairy. The eyes still human in the face of the monster.

He's one of them. I made a mistake coming here.

A huge, freaking mistake.

She whirled and ran for the door, stepping outside, only to freeze at the low growl. A large cat stepped into view from behind the fueling station, green-eyed and vicious-looking, his tawny fur stood up in a ridge along his back. He let out a low rumble of warning.

It wasn't the first time she'd heard it because Kelso, her captor, could change into a giant mountain cat!

She held out her hands. "No. I won't go back."

Kelso advanced, a slow slinking predator who would never let her go.

From behind, another feline pressed her and, stuck between the two, there appeared to be no way out for Dani.

I failed to escape. Again.

Tears pricked her eyes.

"Don't move, darling. I got this," a voice shouted. A moment later, a sharp crack sounded then another. Over five shots fired in total, resulting in two cats racing away, both bleeding heavily.

Someone saved me.

Could anyone hear the angels singing hallelujah? Danita beamed at the man with the smoking gun. "Thank you. Oh, thank you. You have no idea what you've just saved me from."

The older gent tipped his wide-brimmed cowboy hat.

"My pleasure to help, ma'am. Even if you almost took out my grill."

She noticed the large Cadillac behind the elderly cowboy. "Sorry about that. I was trying to escape."

The cowboy hat tipped back, and she could more clearly see his creased and concerned features. "Mountain lions attacking folks. Never seen that before. It's not too safe in these parts."

She shook her head. "No, it's not."

"I don't suppose you need a ride elsewhere?"

As a matter of fact, she did. But could she endanger someone else? "I probably shouldn't." She eyed the dirt bike on the ground and held in a sigh.

"I know a way over the border that doesn't require a passport, if that helps in any way."

Startled, she gaped at him.

His lips quirked into a smile. "Sometimes a man doesn't want the government knowing what he's doing. So, what do you say?"

It seemed stupid to refuse the best offer she'd probably get.

Which was why she got into that Cadillac and hoped she only imagined the enraged scream of a giant cat as the cowboy drove away.

Chapter 2

THE GUITAR SOLO SCREAMED, POURING FROM HIS speakers as Rory drove down the single-lane highway as if the cops were already after him. *I'm a wanted man.* Which was why Rory fled town before anyone could arrest him. To be fair, the cops had good reason for issuing a warrant. He'd committed arson and almost killed someone. Two someones, actually.

But his crime spree didn't end there. Rory had burnt a factory to the ground, put hundreds of people out of work—which he felt bad about. Innocent folk didn't deserve to pay for the sins of his family. His very fucked-up family.

Just how fucked up you might ask? Only recently had he met his real dad, as in the one who seduced his mother and left his son to be raised by another man. The reunion didn't go well—reference the above aforementioned fire. His stepdad was pissed he'd even gone in the first place. His mother was heartbroken he wouldn't leave well enough alone—neglecting the fact he was traumatized to know his mom had sex with another man. Never mind the fact his mother should never, ever have sex.

Ever.

He was an immaculate conception. He was sticking to that.

Could you see his shitty week thus far? And that wasn't even the entirety of it. To top it all off, he'd ditched a fake fiancée—a woman who annoyed with her false airs and grating voice. She, however, didn't appreciate being dumped and expressed her discontent vocally. He could see why she remained single.

He gave them all the finger as he sped out of town.

Given his actions, more than a few people were pissed at him. Was it any wonder he wanted to get as far as he could from the place? Bumfuck, Canada. Nice people, okay place. Lots of fucking trees. He missed the soothing crash of waves slapping against the shore, the sound he woke up to every morning in his beach house on the coast. Not the Californian coast like so many paid too much for, but the Texan one. He liked that everything was bigger there: houses, steaks, and egos.

He also missed the real Rory, the guy who didn't commit crimes. Who wasn't a complete and utter asshole. Something had happened to him when he finally met his bio dad. Something inside him snapped and made him into a jerk he didn't recognize. *Not entirely true. I turned into my dad.* The one who raised him.

Despite worrying about the warrant out for his arrest, Rory drove his rebuilt, red Maserati—a fucking rocket on four wheels—across the border, and when asked what he had to declare, he said, "Nothing." Which was true. He'd left everything, including his self-respect, behind.

He was, however, followed by his bumbling idiot posse. Morons—that he couldn't kill because they were cousins—who'd caused more trouble than they were worth. When they'd said they wanted to accompany Rory so he wouldn't be alone when facing his real father for the first time, he thought they would help keep him grounded and remind him why he'd come out here—to face the man who'd defiled his mother.

His cousins had helped all right. Helped Rory appear as a thug. It was their idea to attack some of the inhabitants in the woods and then light some fires—which were quite pretty—and when the flames licked the vat of syrup, bubbling it, he got damned hungry.

Because of their actions—and constant goading to do something—Rory was running from the law. Which was totally cool in action movies. In real life? A lot more nerve-wracking than a man wanted to deal with.

Which was why, while dealing with the lovely uniformed security woman with the steely gaze at the border, he said, "I don't mean to tattle, but I'm pretty sure the car behind me has contraband." Rory leaned closer and whispered, "I overheard them while having lunch at a diner saying they had the goods and that they would fetch a good price."

"What goods?"

He shrugged. "I don't know, but they each spent a goodly amount of time in the men's room."

"Thanks for the tip, sir." She smiled at him, and he winked.

"My pleasure."

Leaving under the speed limit, and grinning like a loon, Rory hoped this would put an end to his tail. The strip search and anal cavity probe would keep his bumbling posse busy for a while, long enough for him to put some distance between them and indulge in some alone time. Also known as wallowing. He was perfectly fine with wallowing since he had plenty to wallow about.

In a most spectacular fashion, Rory had royally fucked everything up. His life. His self-respect. His possible freedom. And for what? To confront a man who had never even known he'd existed.

The look in Elanroux's eyes when he discovered Rory was his son was too genuine to fake. He'd honestly not known about Rory. Which, in some respects, made his anger worse. Since he couldn't hate his mother—he'd kill the person who did her wrong—he had to hate the two people he held to blame. Elanroux for not keeping it in his pants, and his dad—make that stepdad—who'd lied to him his entire life.

How different would his life have been had he known his bio dad? At thirty years of age, it was too late to find out now. Not to forget he'd ruined any chance of a relationship after what he'd done. *I'm good at burning bridges. Just look at all the people angry with me.*

As if mere thought were a beacon, his phone buzzed yet again. An angry buzz that chided him to answer. Probably his father. Or should he call him stepdad now that he knew the truth? It burned to realize the man who'd raised him—*the man I feared and hero worshipped in equal measure*—wasn't his real father. Rory never even suspected the secret. However, blood didn't lie.

Neither did his parents when confronted. *"We thought it best you never knew."* From his mother. As for his father, he simmered as the truth of his infertility was revealed. He lashed out. *"That's why you're a no-good wastrel."*

At least now he had an explanation for his father's seesawing behavior.

The ignobility of his parentage also gave Rory an excuse for his actions, given his whole world, his entire existence, had gone on a loopy loop.

I don't know who I am anymore. Whose values should he embrace? Who should he look up to and emulate, Daddy one or two? How to apologize to the mother he'd insulted without insulting her again?

There was only one thing to do when a man drowned in a mire of lost identity. Only one place to go where people didn't judge a man who screwed up royally. It took three days of driving with stops only to eat and sleep to reach Nevada.

The moment he turned onto the strip he felt his troubles ease. Las Vegas was the kind of place to make him forget his woes. Everything here was a distraction. The bright flashing lights. The throngs of people constantly in motion. Las Vegas knew how to treat a man like a king—if you had money to burn, which was why Rory chose a lavish hotel with an attached casino.

A valet took care of parking, and once Rory gave his name at the registration desk, they couldn't do enough to please him. The Lupin name opened doors because it meant money. Money to spend. Money to burn. And he could technically tap it on dual sides since both his daddies were loaded rich. Rory already knew his bio dad would give him money. He'd offered. A ton of it to assuage his guilt. However, Rory hadn't gone to meet bio dad for more wealth. He'd wanted a measure of the man who thought it okay to mess around with someone's wife.

Cheating was never okay. If a man found himself unhappy at home, then he needed to move on, and vice versa for a woman. Not that Rory ever intended to settle with a single woman.

The very idea of being with only one person forever was kind of horrifying, actually. One pussy for life? Just one more reason to never tie the knot and get hitched. He'd much rather play the field and move on when he got bored.

What about kids?

As his stepdad's only son—even if by marriage—and his bio dad's only living heir, if you ignored his annoying nephew, then Rory was under some pressure to produce someone to carry on the name.

But he could worry about that problem another day. Right now, he was more than content to sit in the VIP lounge, sipping on a cocktail. Then two. Then three. A nice buzz was just what he needed.

On his trip back from the men's room—where he made room for the next round of cocktails—he saw her.

More like sensed her. A magnetic pull and then a moment of "hot damn." If he'd been wearing a tail, he would have thumped it.

As to what caught his eye? A hot thing in slim-fitting jeans, a shirt tucked loosely into them, and brunette hair halfway down her back.

Smells yummy. His inner dog—a real canine, as in a wolf and not the douche canoe version—perked up at the smell of her.

Rory perked up, too. Nothing like the sweet embrace of a woman to forget all his woes. He raked his fingers through his hair, smoothed his beard, making sure nothing was caught, and then sauntered in her direction. He casually leaned against the machine she was playing.

"Hey, good—"

"Not happening. Go away." Said flatly without her even turning to look.

Undaunted, he took a moment to stare at her, the fine features of her face, the scent of her, all human and delicious. What did she bathe in? Because he just wanted to rub and roll against her. To mix his scent with hers.

"I don't think I've ever seen you around here." Perfectly true if inane. Thousands of people went through this casino in short periods of time.

"Go away," she repeated, her gaze still locked on her screen. She pulled with grim determination. Not a bit of enjoyment. A true gambler? Those were a dangerous breed. They'd risk it all for a game.

I gambled. And now what do I have? The beginnings of a stunning drunk, a hot chick who thought she could shoot him down, an ego currently around his ankles and still sinking. He'd lost so much, and he was quite lit, which was why he didn't back off. "What if I said, no, I'm not leaving? It's a public place. I can stand where I like. And I like it right here." He added a charming smile to ensure she understood the compliment.

Finally, her head turned that she could shoot him a glare. "What part of 'not interested' are you not grasping?"

Shot down? Only one thing to do. Pretend she misunderstood. "Are you implying I'm hitting on you?"

"You're leaning on my machine."

"Just waiting my turn, sweet cheeks." He winked.

"Then you'll be waiting awhile. I am not leaving until this thing pays out, which will be any time now." She yanked the handle, and the gears inside spun, flashing colors and symbols. Different ones came to a stop. No money.

She went at it again. Her gaze once again locked. Ignoring him.

"You here alone?" he asked.

"Is this an attempt to gauge how long before someone will miss me after you kidnap me and sell me on the black market?"

He blinked. "Uh, no. just wondering if you have a linebacker boyfriend or husband who might show up and knock me out."

"I do. The hugest. Now go away."

"I think you're lying."

"And I think you're harassing me. Give me some space."

"How's this?" He moved closer by an inch.

She uttered a heavy sigh as she yanked the handle again.

Another loss and he could see her pile of coins dwindling in her lap.

"You play here often?" he asked. It wouldn't surprise him to find out she was a gambler. Too many people had a gambling vice. They didn't know when to walk away. Some people called it an addiction. The last time he was here with cousin Byron, he claimed he gambled for his retirement—a plan that thus far had him retiring to live in a cardboard box.

As for Rory? He saw gambling as a way to needle his dad, who thought all forms of wagering were a colossal waste of time and money.

She didn't reply.

Undaunted, Rory took the seat beside her and swiped a card in the machine instead of using coins. She kept ignoring him as she pulled. He yanked the lever, knowing full well it wasn't a true gear system slot machine anymore. Everything had gone electronic, but people wanted the thrill of the old style game. The yanking of levers rather than just a slight tap of a screen.

Old or new, the machines invariably took more than they paid. The spinning stopped. They were both losers.

They tried again.

A waitress walked by, and Rory snapped his fingers. "A whiskey sour for me and a..." He looked at the woman.

She didn't reply. Big surprise.

"Something feminine for the lady."

The woman obviously wasn't ignoring him as much as she pretended because she snorted. "You just don't give up, do you?"

Tenaciousness was one of his better traits. "I'm like a wolf with a bone." His mother had kept the dinosaur one she'd gotten him as a cub. The edges of it gnawed. He'd slept with that thing for a few years. One day he'd...have no son to give it to. The idea made him frown.

"Wolf, bear. Doesn't matter. My daddy used to hunt. He taught me how, too."

How intriguing. "Used to? Does your father not hunt anymore?"

"My father's dead." Spoken bluntly.

It roused soft words. "I'm sorry."

"So am I."

For a moment, they played in silence, or at least without conversation, given the hum of noise all around from voices, machines, and bells.

She won a small pile, which drew a heavy sigh. She kept plunking in coins and pulling.

"You know, these cheaper machines don't pay out as often as the ones with a higher chip-in amount."

"Maybe not, but if I'm going to lose, I want it to take time rather than be broke in just a minute."

"Such pessimism. Why gamble if you don't enjoy it?"

"Because I don't have a choice." She turned away and yanked.

"This is the casino I come to when life gets to be too much and I need to unwind."

She didn't ask the obvious question.

They played a few more rounds before he remarked, "Your pile of coins is getting small." A glance over showed her tiny bucket almost empty.

"Yeah, I know." She sighed. "Here I thought my luck was finally turning. Guess I was wrong."

"Wrong about what?" he prodded, then said nothing more. He thought she wouldn't answer.

"Wrong about everything." The tone was self-deprecating, which Rory could totally understand. Which was why he offered her a second drink when he ordered his. She'd downed the first one.

"Tell me about yourself," he said, sipping and feeling the line of fire as the whiskey burned its way down.

"You don't mean that."

"I asked, didn't I?"

She slanted her gaze at him. "As part of your ploy to get in my pants. We both know you don't give a hoot about me. You're just playing Mr. Nice Guy so I'll have sex with you."

"You make me sound so mercenary."

"I would have said rakish."

"That sounds better."

"Not really. I've met your type before. Pushy. Arrogant. Only interested in one thing."

"You're right, I am." He tipped his glass at her and drained it before saying, "I do love giving pleasure."

"Your hand must get awful tired." She said it with a

straight face; therefore, it took a moment to sink in. When it did, he laughed. A dry sense of humor. The kind he could appreciate.

He paused to look at her more closely, especially her ring finger. "Are you seeing someone or married?"

"Do you really care?" She cast him a sideways glance before she shoved her last coin into the slot. He could see her lips move in a silent prayer before she yanked the lever.

Whir. Clink. Clink. Clink. Clink. The machine spat realistic sounds. Another loss and her shoulders slumped. "So much for changing my luck," she said.

"Luck is a crutch for those who don't work hard." At her pointed look, he shrugged. "Or so my dad says."

"What do you think?" she asked.

"I think sometimes luck is all you have. Here." He pulled a coin out of his pocket. He kissed it before handing it over.

"You really think smooching a heap of metal will make it lucky?" She arched a brow.

"Try it and see."

"This is stupid," she muttered, but she dropped the coin into the slot and reached to yank on the handle.

The machine whirred and spun. *Clink. Clink.* One by one the tokens stopped. Another loss.

She smirked at him. "Guess you're not that lucky either."

"That's because what you needed was a real kiss."

A snort left her. "That was exceptionally cheesy."

"A little."

"A lot," she said, draining her second glass of something blue.

A waitress whisked by and replaced both their glasses.

"Let's try it again." He pulled out a new coin and held it up. "But this time. You let me kiss you. For luck."

"I don't kiss strangers."

"My name is Rory."

"This is crazy. A kiss won't make me lucky." She twirled the stem of the glass in her hands, not meeting his gaze.

"You don't know that for certain. Pucker up, darling."

"Darling?" she repeated with a wrinkle of her nose.

"Would you prefer baby girl?"

"No. I'm no baby. I'll bet I'm almost as tall as you." She took a sip before setting her drink down and standing.

He stood quickly, too, the pair of them close to eye level. Very close. The scent of her swirled around him.

Hunger rumbled. Not the kind that wanted food.

"How tall are you?" he murmured, staring into her eyes, the hazel irises flecked with gold. Captivating.

"Five nine."

"And I'm just shy of six foot."

"My daddy was taller."

"I'm tall enough." He stepped closer, the whiskey obviously stronger than expected, given the lightheadedness her nearness made him feel. The heat of her radiated, and yet it couldn't compare to the raging fire inside him.

"What are you doing?"

"Giving you luck." Even if he'd lacked any of late. Perhaps by kissing her, he'd find it again.

"I never said you could kiss me."

"Scared?"

"I'm not frightened by you."

"Prove it," he dared her. Expected another rebuttal. Maybe even a slap for being so intense.

Instead, she pressed her mouth to his.

And his senses exploded.

Chapter 3

WHAT AM I DOING? SHE WAS KISSING A MAN, A stranger, and why?

Because he'd dared her.

Yet, it wasn't just that. This guy, who said his name was Rory, looked good—as in dressed in a suit, tall, blondish with a short, sexy beard—and he smelled divine.

He tasted even better. Like super delicious. And gosh darn it, the kiss felt incredible. The slant of his mouth over hers stealing her breath. When was the last time she'd done something pleasurable for herself? And before anyone got on her case about being too free with her affection, this was the 2000s, a time when women owned their bodies and their sexuality. If she wanted to screw a man, she would.

And she'd damned well enjoy it. Just not here and now.

She pulled away from him, her lips tingling. She plucked the coin still in his hand and turned to the machine. More to compose herself than because she actually wanted to play.

Therefore, it was with a blank expression that she stared as the symbols clinked into place. One, two, three... It took the dinging bell and the raining sound of coins for her to realize.

"Holy shit, I won!" She numbly looked at the ticket that spat out of the machine, exhorting her to visit a cashier to claim the grand sum of eight thousand, four hundred eighty-three dollars. Enough to keep her going for a while.

"What did I tell you, darling? My kiss brings good luck."

A smile finally tugged her lips. "I guess it did. Thanks." She peeked at him and noted the squareness of his jaw even through his trimmed golden beard. He was good-looking, tall, and just her type, if she had a type, but she was staying away from men for the moment.

"How about you thank me by having dinner." He uttered the request in a deep baritone that did quivery things to her insides.

She knew where he hoped dinner would lead. "I'm still not sleeping with you," she stated.

"I'm not asking you to. Have a meal with me. Just a meal, nothing else."

The right thing to do? Grab her winnings and go. She'd gotten what she came for. But...When was the last time she'd enjoyed flirting with a man? Felt that tummy-tingling warmth that came from sexual attraction?

"I might be hungry for a steak dinner, a good one, with all the fixings."

"I know just the place. And their wine selection is quite good, too."

She'd long since exchanged her track suit for other clothing. When she'd first escaped with her cowboy companion—who'd introduced himself as Cody—he'd stopped, allowing her to shop. He didn't ask many questions, which she appreciated. Kept offering to help. Said his wife kept a spare room.

She almost said yes. But even though the tough Texan carried a gun, she just couldn't bring herself to accept his help. What if Kelso found her? Her kind Samaritan could have gotten hurt, which was why she'd said goodbye to Cody the cowboy two days ago.

A lonely two days. A bus brought her south, a long uncomfortable trip that left her wallet dry and her ass sore. She'd just about given up when she'd seen the bright lights.

Now look at her, free from Kelso, still running, flush with cash, and in Vegas with a handsome man who wanted to buy her dinner.

"Let's go." She couldn't have said who was more surprised.

The red liquid flowed down her throat too easily. The food melted in her mouth. The check the casino gave her in exchange for her ticket kept her warm inside her bra.

Over the course of the meal, she learned about her good-luck kisser. His name was Rory Beauchamp, and he was rich, which she kind of figured. In an expected cliché, Rory had some serious daddy issues, but on the flip side, he kissed like a god.

No, seriously, he did. Ever since that embrace she'd not been able to stop thinking of it, and the many glasses of wine didn't help, nor did the intimate booth and low lighting of the restaurant.

"You're staring at me again," she remarked, taking a sip to hide her trembling. Her observation didn't stop him in the least. And the wine did nothing to calm her nerves. Every part of her was awake. Alert.

He shrugged, wide shoulders wearing a proper button-up shirt but a very loose tie. He'd draped the jacket on the seat beside him. An elegant yuppie dining with a trailer park girl in jeans and a T-shirt. She wondered if he'd had to bribe the maître d' to ignore her ensemble. This place definitely had a dress code.

Which was why she snorted when Rory said, "I can't help staring at you. You're gorgeous."

"I'm a hot mess. Especially compared to the other diners."

"You're naturally pretty."

"You're drunk."

"Not that much."

"I am." She knew it because she didn't move away when he slid closer.

"If I'm inebriated, it's because you intoxicate me." He leaned in close and nuzzled her, his nose buried in her hair as he breathed her scent in. "You're not a real brunette, are you?" he noted aloud.

Had her roots begun to show already? "Does it matter?"

"Not really. Just most women tend to become blonde, not the other way around."

"I'm not most women."

"I've noticed." He sat close, his thigh pressing along hers. She jumped when his hand came to rest on her knee.

"Where are you staying?"

"Nowhere." She chose to drink more wine rather than think about the fingers tickling up her leg.

I should move his hand. She didn't want to, though. His touch felt nice. She quivered. As in a quiver down *there*. When was the last time that happened?

Long enough that she didn't want the shivery sensation to stop.

"I have a room big enough for two."

"That wouldn't be proper." Neither was his hand resting on her mound, the heel of it pressing against her, creating a pleasurable friction.

"I want you."

Bold words.

"I can't." Actually, she could. What exactly stopped her?

Her breath hitched as he kept rubbing.

His lips tickled the lobe of her ear. "I've never wanted a woman as bad as I want you."

"It's the wine talking." Spoken almost in a whisper, yet she understood what he meant. Something about him, this moment, had her acting so boldly. Since when did desire overcome control?

Since I realized life is too short to waste. Let her take one selfish moment of fun. Her eyes closed, and her head tilted back, silent permission for him to continue. And he did. His fingers pressed and rubbed, causing such a delightful friction.

His mouth moved against her hair, a silken skein over her ear, and yet she still felt his hot breath when he whispered, "Touch me and see how much I crave you."

She didn't mean to, and yet her hand ended up cupping his groin. The turgid length of him bulged, begging for release.

She needed release. He kept stroking. Faster and faster. Her breathing hitched, and she almost screamed when a clatter of dishes falling startled her. Her eyes flashed open, she noted a couple walking by, the woman chin high and disapproving, her companion looking at them.

Heat burnt her cheeks.

Oh my God, what am I doing?

"I have to go." She shoved away from him and fled the booth. But she'd misjudged how much she'd drunk. The wine she'd imbibed hit her hard. She blinked and wavered but kept moving. One foot in front of the other, the people around a mere blur, as she headed for the doors to the casino. Pushing through them, she took only a few paces before hitting a wall of smoke.

Damn the Vegas laws on indoor smoking. She'd chosen a far empty corner to play before, close to an air return system, but to exit the hotel she'd have to go straight through it. She realized that, while she'd dined the multicourse meal she only vaguely remembered, time had passed. The afternoon crowd had given way to the evening one. Unlike the daytimers, these were more about the party.

The booze flowed all around. Glowing tips of cigarettes sparked like hanging red stars in the air. Smoke. So much smoke. She couldn't exactly hold her breath, which meant she got to inhale a lungful of tobacco. She saw an exit sign and headed for it. She shoved through the door and startled a group of people. The guy holding the water bong lifted his gaze to look at her but never let his suction on the glass loosen.

Smoking drugs obviously, but not the skunky weed. She whiffed something else. Something with a sweetly acrid aftertaste. It tickled her nose, and she meant to hold her breath, but someone from behind brushed past her, and she opened her mouth with an inhaled gasp. She immediately coughed and sucked in more. Then coughed again.

"Fuck me, smoking that shit in the casino. Get out of here," Rory snapped, his voice firm and welcome given her world spun.

He wrapped an arm around her, and she leaned into his strength while she waited for everything to stop spinning.

A strange lethargy imbued her.

"They were doing drugs," she remarked, her tongue thick in her mouth.

"Yes. But we only got it second hand. It shouldn't be too bad."

For some reason, she smiled. "I actually feel good. Really good." He peeked down at her as the door closed and the last of the smokers fled. The two of them stood in the cloud left behind.

"We should probably move, too."

"In a minute." She turned into him, facing him, and stared. "Why did you follow me?"

"Just wanted to make sure you got where you were going safely."

"Acting as my bodyguard?"

"I was thinking more like a gentleman."

"I don't think you're a gentleman," she stated. Not with that big body of his. Only a few inches taller maybe, but definitely thicker. And all man.

She brushed against him, the jolt of awareness making him suck a deep breath.

"Your eyes are gorgeous." She couldn't help her fascination. They were a blue-gray, and almost lit from within.

"You shouldn't stare at me like that," he replied in a low rumble.

"Why not?"

"Because it stirs the beast."

A laugh escaped her. What was it with men that they gave their penises names? Then again, he did seem kind of primal at the moment. His lower body leaned into her, his hips pinning her. Definite erection, then again, her wet panties were a lady-boner equivalent. His free hand cupped the back of her head.

"What are you doing?"

"Thinking of kissing you."

"Only thinking?" she taunted. She played with fire, she knew it the moment his mouth slanted over hers, but she didn't care. Not anymore.

Everything inside her glowed. She felt so damned good. She laughed with ease. Exactly why was this wrong?

It certainly didn't feel wrong when he kissed and ground against her, rousing her passion so expertly she had a mini orgasm right there on the wall.

A part of her understood they were drunk, and something more. Something in that leftover smoke that made them both lower their inhibitions. Perhaps that explained how Rory didn't notice someone exiting the casino right as he stuck his hand down her pants, cupping her bare ass.

"We need to find another spot," she mumbled. Not, "Let's stop." No "Hey, what are you thinking?" She wanted this as much as he did.

"Anything my mate desires." Rory's arm around her waist guided her. They returned to the casino, were offered shots of tequila—three of them—as they were on the way to somewhere, she couldn't quite recall. The last thing she clearly remembered him saying was, "I've got an idea."

After that things were fuzzy. Okay, truthfully, she didn't recall anything, which was why her very hungover head remained lying face down on the pillow, a pillow she didn't remember hitting. Her gritty eyes opened, and she saw a head. Shortish blond hair. Big body. And she was curled around it.

Naked.

What did I do?

Waking next to a stranger with a pasty taste in her mouth wasn't exactly her idea of making good choices. Then again, she'd not made any brilliant ones from the moment she'd kissed Rory. Which made her wonder, was he the one in bed with her?

God, I hope so. She didn't remember anyone else. Given she did recollect some necking, it seemed likely he'd managed to get her into bed. A pity she couldn't remember it, but he was obviously good. Her body held a splendid languor. Her lips were full and obviously well kissed. And she had an arm tossed over his body and her lower area curved around his.

Waking to find herself spooning a man. There was a first.

She moved slowly, slipping away her arm. For a moment, he stopped breathing. So did she.

She waited, not wanting to wake him. Because then he'd want to talk. Or do other things. She didn't have time for other things. She'd already lingered too long.

He resumed snoring softly, and she couldn't help but stare at him, the daylight filtering through the curtains showing it wasn't just the booze making him as handsome as she recalled. The smooth skin of his back tempted her to touch.

She tucked her hand away and resisted. No more dallying. She had the money, no reason to stick around.

Time to find her stuff and get going. Especially her bra with the check!

She slid from the bed, her naked body protesting the chill air conditioning of the room. It proved easy to spot their path from the night before. The trail of clothes began at the door. She found the casino check inches from her bra on the floor.

Alongside some blinking antennas.

What the hell did we do?

Naked things, obviously. She wore not a stitch. Her bag had made it to the room, which meant she had a fresh change of clothes. The yoga pants more for comfort than appearance. The bra plain cotton. She dug a new pair of underpants from her bag. Wincing as the plastic packaging they were still in crinkled.

He didn't move.

The breath she held eased out. She hit the bathroom for a quick visit. Washing her hands at the sink, she glanced in the mirror. Disheveled hair? To be expected. Full lips from kissing. Obviously a sign she'd had a good time. The bite mark on her neck? Definitely more than a hickey.

What did he do? She leaned forward to see it better, the perfect crescent mark of his teeth in her skin colored in blood. "Son of a bitch," she breathed.

She was totally tempted to give him a piece of her mind, but then that would mean talking to him, and in the light of day, she couldn't believe what she'd done.

Exiting the bathroom, she noted him still sprawled asleep. She gathered her dirty apparel and stuffed it into the bag while the check went back into her bra. Finished dressing, she had her bag in hand about to tiptoe out of his room when she saw them tossed carelessly alongside a wallet. Car keys.

Don't do it.

She needed wheels.

She cast a peek over her shoulder to where he snored. She really shouldn't. He'd been nothing but nice to her.

Only so he could get what he wanted.

In all fairness, I wanted it too.

Surely, he wouldn't begrudge helping her.

He owed her even for biting her. It might leave a scar.

Sorry.

She snatched the keys and ran.

Chapter 4

IT HAD BEEN OVER A WEEK SINCE HIS CAR WAS stolen in Vegas. A perfect way to cap off a perfectly shitty month. It didn't help that his ego took a bruising when he awoke alone, the woman whose name he couldn't recall, but whose face haunted his dreams, gone.

He should have been happy she didn't stick around to make a scene. Many of the women he'd met in his life, impressed by his status and wealth, tended to cling. Some even resorted to blackmail when guilt tripping didn't work. Not the woman with the captivating scent and no name. She fled without a goodbye, leaving not a single trace, and in his fucking car!

After the week he'd had, he hit rock bottom.

Which meant there was only one direction to go. Back up. Rory needed to find the positive, starting with the bet he'd lost. As part of his stupid plan to make his bio daddy pay, he'd agreed to marry and impregnate a woman in order to inherit. In his defense, the payout was huge. As in billions huge.

Still, though, a ball and chain at his delicate age? He was on the cusp of thirty. Still a pup with so many doggy fucking years left.

What if I don't want to get tied down? Rory wasn't the type to ever want to settle with just one lady, which meant he silently cheered when he lost the bet. Although he'd made a good show of it. The charade had gone on for ridiculously long. A fake engagement that created a sticky situation with Chanice, a woman who seemed to think their bogus engagement was real. She called. Texted. Showed up uninvited to his room. It got embarrassing how much she tried to trap him.

He hated clingy.

He also hated the fact the woman, who'd left the most amazing scent on his hotel sheets and stolen his fucking car, had disappeared and didn't return. He knew because he waited for her.

Spent a few extra days playing, switching to roulette when he tired of the slots. Won tons of money he didn't need. Drank his face off, too. During that time he kept an eye open for the woman. Kept hoping he'd catch her scent. At the same time, he couldn't muster any interest in anyone else of the opposite sex. The only thing that penetrated his partying fog was that his car was recovered in some Texas border town, stripped of everything but the frame. With the tires gone, they'd left the sad carcass sitting on milk crates. It was a slapping reminder his car thief wasn't coming back.

For some reason, that bothered him. It bothered him still several days after his return home, the one he'd gotten on the Texas coast. A home that seemed too big and quiet.

Lonely.

He'd not told anyone he was here yet. Not even his mother. He wasn't done with the whole wallowing thing yet. But at least he'd stopped drinking. Booze never solved anything. And his recycling bins were full.

He lived in a neighborhood that still received door-to-door mail, a dying service in a digitally advancing age.

It was shoved through the slot in the door, hitting the floor. Mostly junk—flyers with big banners declaring sales. But amongst the pile was a large, purple envelope sprinkled in stars. What the hell was that?

He wandered over, coffee mug in hand, and crouched to grab it.

The return address was a PO Box in Vegas. And it was clearly addressed to him. It took only a moment to tear the end open and pull out a booklet on some kind of alien cult religion that involved people dressed in googly eyes around a giant blob. A welcome letter. And finally, an invoice for a quickie marriage done at the Chapel of Latter Day Aliens.

Blink.

It must be a mistake. He checked the name and address. His. The information on the groom. His. The bride? Some random chick named Danita DuMoines.

What. The. Fuck.

He might not remember much from that night—though

assumed some flesh-pounding fun that left him sticky—and had only a vague recollection of yelling, "I fucking do."

Oh shit, what did I do?

According to this bill for services, he'd gotten married. No way. Not with his phobia. This had to be some sick joke, or mistake.

There was a number on the form. It invited a person to log onto their website and check out the wedding pictures.

Moving with robotic-like jerkiness, Rory sat in a chair and flipped open his laptop. He punched in the address for the website. A bright image appeared of a huge saucer, porthole windows dotting it, floating over an Earth city. A light beamed down, and a happy couple in a gown and suit were being beamed up to it.

Mouth dry, he clicked the link on the top right, the one saying: View the Star Logs.

Enter your code.

He tapped it. Hit Enter.

Let out a relived sigh when it said: *Invalid Code. Check your receipt and try again.*

He almost shut it down, but thought, *maybe I should check the code.* A frown creased his brow as he realized he'd typed H instead of B. He changed it. Hit Enter.

Squeaked.

Like a mouse.

Not a man.

Or a wolf.

He wasn't even a dog in that moment.

Say hello to the lumpy meatball in the chair staring at the blurry yet recognizable image of himself on screen, dressed in a suit, buttoned lopsided, a stupid grin plastered to his face. At his side, an altar glowing with neon lights and a person dressed in a Star Lord costume, hands folded.

Means nothing.

He clicked for the next image.

A blurry shot of a woman, at least it seemed like a woman, with an hourglass shape in pants and a shirt, holding...what the fuck was she holding? And what about her face? The blurry blob told him nothing.

Click.

She came into stark relief, a brunette with hair scraped back in a ponytail, her expression out of focus, her lips pink. She wore a T-shirt, a simple blue one, tucked into jeans. She clutched a bouquet of bobbing antennas with blinking eyeballs on the tips.

Next.

They stood together, both of them smiling widely. Obviously happy in that moment.

Because she smelled so good. His wolf was the one to remind him. He wouldn't have married a woman because of her scent.

I married a nice-smelling car thief.

Next.

They faced each other at the altar, hands clasped, staring intently.

Her eyes are chocolate pools I could drown in.

She's obviously some kind of scammer who takes advantage of men.

Next.

Their lips brushed.

It was like electricity. Every time they touched, it jolted him.

How much of that was because of the booze and drugs? He recalled the copious amounts of alcohol and the sugary sweet scent of opium in the stairwell, one of the few drugs that could get even a shapeshifter high.

Were drugs to blame for his intense recollection of the woman? He certainly held it to blame for him spilling his sad story of two daddies, which she giggled about and declared false. Then tried to one-up him with a tale of being kidnapped and escaping some freak who was holding her hostage because her daddy owed him something.

Obviously untrue. More likely she was a prostitute looking for some extra cash. She had, after all, stolen his car—*yet she left my wallet full of cash.* Probably after a bigger prize. Well, if she thought this fake wedding was going to net her dollars, she was sadly mistaken.

The tart wouldn't get a damned thing from him. Not one single penny.

Rory rang his lawyer. "I need you to annul a wedding for me," he stated without preamble when Connor answered. His best friend since high school, Connor, along with their Johnny and Freddy, were a squad who knew they could count on each other no matter what.

"Ever think of trying this thing called, 'Hello. How's it going? Long time no talk.'?"

"This is an emergency. Some gold digger fooled me into getting hitched. I need you to reverse it."

A snicker came through the ear piece of his phone. "You got married. Mr. Never-In-A-Million-Years? That's fucking priceless."

"I was drunk."

"Apparently. Which will help when I file. I assume you were too wasted to consummate."

"I—" *He sank into her, and she dug her nails into his back, urging him on.* "We might have screwed. Once. No more." That he recalled, but once or three times, it didn't matter.

"Then you are shit out of luck on the annulment, my friend. You'll have to go the divorce route."

"For a woman I barely remember?"

"Don't yell at me. I don't make the laws."

"I thought there was a law against letting people get married drunk."

"Where did you get married?"

"Vegas."

Snicker.

Rory growled. "That's not helping."

"Don't get pissy with me. I'm not the moron who got wasted and married."

"You have to fix this."

"I'll do what I can. Send the info you have on this broad and I'll get the paperwork started on the divorce."

Except that wasn't straightforward either. The

address she'd filled out on the form proved to be false, and a search of her name in databases—even ones he shouldn't have access to—didn't show anything.

For all intents and purposes, his supposed wife didn't exist.

It should have relieved him. A woman this hard to find probably wanted nothing to do with him. Had probably forgotten, or wanted to forget, what they'd done. He certainly did.

Then why did he keep having dreams of her?

Why did his wolf whine and urge him to find her? *She needs me.* He couldn't shake the feeling, yet could do nothing about it.

But that didn't stop him from searching.

Chapter 5

WHAT AM I DOING? DANI'S PLAN INVOLVED GETTING through customs to Mexico and then farther south still. That was her plan, except once she neared the border, she'd gotten nervous. What would she do down there? She didn't speak Spanish. She had barely any money. Nothing to her name but a knapsack of clothes and a marriage certificate found stuffed in the bottom days after she fled Las Vegas.

How could I have done that?

She was on the lam. She had to keep moving lest Kelso find her, and yet, she couldn't help but look at that piece of paper, the one declaring her Mrs. Beauchamp. A legal and binding tie. Was it fair to Rory that she skip out and leave him tied?

Because, as far as she knew, the law wouldn't grant a divorce without her signature, and the sex they'd had made annulment out of the question.

Unless he lies. A man like him probably would have no problem telling a court that nothing happened.

She had nothing to worry about. Yet...what if she were wrong? What if the marriage was binding? One day he might want to get married for real. Or maybe she would. Then what?

It meant that, instead of heading to Mexico as planned, she tracked him down in his hometown. The address on the car ownership papers in the glovebox something she'd partially memorized. Who could forget an exotic address like Seawall Boulevard in Galveston, Texas? And the number, of course, one sixty-nine.

He lived out of her flight path, and yet she found herself here with no real plan. She'd never watched a movie that could give her a tip on this. Exactly what should a woman do? Show up on his doorstep and demand a divorce? He'd probably readily agree. But what if...what if he didn't? What if he wanted a real marriage? Or he was angry? Men could take offense at many things. Especially one who felt he might have been wronged.

Kelso had a violent temper. Her saving grace was he'd needed her alive.

But Rory might prefer her dead.

The worry and doubt and, yes, even the feelings of guilt ran in circles inside her head. All of her instincts told her to move on and forget him, forget about the piece of paper saying she was his wife.

But she couldn't.

Is it because you can't forget how he made you feel? After their initial rough start, she'd warmed to him.

The Wolf's Secret Vegas Bride

Warmed to his charm. Laughed at his absurd claims of having two fathers and a soap opera life. Their attraction was mutual and fierce. She'd tried to fight it, telling him she wasn't the type of girl to indulge in sex lightly. But he'd pursued her, and perhaps it was the alcohol or drugs talking, but for some reason, she recalled him saying he'd known from the moment he smelled her—yes, smelled, not saw—that she was his mate.

His woman. And the way Rory said it, his expression alight with a primal wildness, intent and truthful, she'd believed it. Wanted it.

Who knew if it was real or imagined? All she could state with any degree of certainty was he'd left a mark on her. One that couldn't be washed clean and hopefully didn't leave human rabies. Who the hell bit hard enough to break skin? For that alone he deserved she take his damned car. At least when she left it at the truck stop, she'd placed a note with the key so it could be returned to him. At that point, she fled by foot then bus, making her way farther south, almost to the Mexican border.

She spent the night in a small town before hitching a ride, which was as dangerous as it sounded. Yet what choice did she have? There were no buses running to Galveston and she wasn't spending any of her earnings on renting a car. She lucked out and made it alive. The burly female driver let her off at a gas station. Dani walked a few blocks until she reached a street with grand houses, closely built together, towering beach homes.

A street for rich folk.

She didn't have the nerve to march up to his door and

knock. What would she say? *Hi, I'm your Vegas bride. I want a divorce.* Yet, at the same time, she didn't. Which made no sense. All Dani knew was meeting Rory, the parts she remembered at least, was fun. Exciting. Waking to his solid body? Not exactly horrifying. What would it be like to wake beside the same person every day?

To not live in fear. To not be alone. She used to remember how that felt, but nowadays, she only knew how to run and look over her shoulder.

She peered at the house. A solid house, old enough to have weathered storms. Like her old house, the one she shared with her daddy. A Craftsman style, with a wide porch and woodwork all over. Old floors that creaked when she walked and her bed on the second floor, with the ceiling slanted to match the pitch of the roof. The window seat was where her father snuggled her and read her stories at night.

Sniffle. It still seemed surreal to think he was gone. It didn't help being on the run. She'd had little time to truly grieve. *Because I don't want to believe he's gone.*

A part of her held out the hope that Kelso had lied. That her father lived and was simply detained. Perhaps he was home right now. Wondering where she was.

I could go home. If only she could.

Impossible. Just like remaining married to a stranger would never work even if her heart raced a mile a minute at the prospect of seeing him again.

Don't get confused. It would be easy to let the attraction overwhelm. It was too dangerous for them both. Kelso would never understand. He'd see her marriage to

Rory as a direct challenge. He had very little control over his rage. He'd let the monster out to shred them as punishment.

If only you were still here, Daddy. However, the safety she'd come to depend on was gone. *I'm on my own.* Sure, he'd not always been there when she was growing up. His business trips kept him away more often than not, but she knew she could count on him.

With the loss of her rock, she faced the world alone.

A heavy sigh left her, and she turned from the house and shifted her backpack higher on her shoulder. She headed down the road, recalling the motel she'd seen on her way in. With her Vegas winnings, she had more than enough for a night. She could use a soft bed and a shower.

The several miles took her the better part of the afternoon to walk as the sun beat down on her head. She was a sweaty, parched mess by the time she arrived at the dingy hotel office, and in no mood to look for another hotel, even though the price tag was more than she liked to pay. She was trying to be stingy with her winnings. They wouldn't last long, and she still hadn't reached her final destination.

Once she checked in, the shower proved well worth it. Standing under the spray, she thirstily drank, her head tilted back, mouth wide open, letting it pour into her mouth. Only once the dryness left her tongue did she turn to let the spray soothe her tired and aching muscles.

The relief was short-lived. All that lovely water she drank? Promptly thrown up.

Her body rebelled and heaved every single drop. The

spasms left her shivering and hunched on the floor of the tub, watching the mess swirl down the drain.

I'm so tired. Tired of running. Tired of hiding. It would just be so much easier to...

Nope. Dani didn't need to hear her father's voice —*only cowards quit*—to know that wasn't the solution. She'd not done her best to escape so that she could give up now. She was free. And yes, things were hard right now, maybe even impossible seeming, but she would find a way to prevail.

She had to.

Wrapped in a towel, she made her way from the bathroom to the bed and collapsed. She fell asleep almost instantly, only to suddenly come awake at a noise.

What the heck? She couldn't tell if her dream startled her, or something else.

Her eyes opened, and she saw only darkness. Her room on the backside of the motel didn't have the glaring neon of the street to peek through the thick blackout curtains.

Rolling over, she noted the alarm clock on the nightstand showing the wee morning hour of three a.m. Way too early, and yet she was wide awake.

Great.

Some drunk must have made a noise, staggering back to his room after the bars closed. She snuggled deeper under the heavy brocade-style comforter, the air conditioning set to an arctic sixty-eight degrees, and inhaled. A faint hint of bleach scented the sheets, but she didn't mind. She liked feeling clean.

Dani closed her eyes and did her best to find that dark hole of sleep that so often eluded her.

Snuffle.

Her eyes shot open at the odd sound. *What was that?*

She held her breath and listened. Only the hum of the air conditioner filled the air. *Click.* It shut off as it reached ambient temperature, and a white noise filled her ears. Which made it easy for her to hear it again, louder and more distinctive this time.

Snuffle. A noise that reminded her of a hound sniffing a trail. Or, in this case, an animal outside her door, nosing his way around.

Probably a raccoon. They loved cities with all their garbage treasures.

But did Texas have raccoons?

Snuffle.

The only thing she could be sure of was it wasn't a bear. Bears didn't roam the city. But what of wild cats that weren't really cats?

Oh my God. Did Kelso and his crew find me?

The very idea had her slipping out of bed, still naked, the towel under the sheets a lumpy, damp mess.

In the dark, she fumbled around for her clothes. Her fingers groped and found her bag. She quickly pulled out items and began slipping them on in the dark. Putting on her pants, she hit the edge of the dresser, causing it to rap against the wall, the noise sharp in the silence. She paused, one leg in her pants, one leg out, and, once again, held her breath.

Did someone hear? She strained to listen. Heard nothing.

A noisy gust of air left her.

I'm being silly. Kelso isn't outside. How could he find her? She'd been careful about not leaving a trail. Hadn't used any cards that could be traced. Never used her real name.

Except for that wedding. For some reason, she'd used all her real information when filling in the license information.

But surely that wasn't common knowledge? Then again, with the Internet nowadays, who could tell?

It's not Kelso. And even if it were, she was in a locked room. He couldn't get in, and if he tried, why, she had a phone on the nightstand. She'd call nine-one-one. Or animal control.

With that thought bolstering her, she flipped on the lamp by the bed, blinking in the sudden bright light.

The room still looked the same, done in a teal color scheme with dark, woven furniture meant to feel beachy but instead looked cheap and worn.

She finished pulling on her pants. Then she found her bra and hooked it on. A T-shirt next. She had her shoes in hand when she heard the weird snuffling noise again. She almost lost control of her bladder when she saw the handle to the door into her room turning.

The door rattled, but held. Not an animal outside after all.

She dove over the bed and reached for the phone. Dead air met her ear. Did she need to dial a number for an outside line? She jabbed the number nine. Then the pound symbol followed by every single damned number to try and get a dial tone. Nothing. Not even the zero worked to connect her to the front desk. The door shook again.

"Go away!" she muttered. Then louder. "Go away. I called the cops. They'll be here any second."

No one replied. The door stopped rattling.

Fear kept her heart pounding. Would the person on the other side of the portal leave? Perhaps they'd stumbled to the wrong room and even now went off in search of the right one.

She didn't dare check out of the window to see. She felt better once she'd wrenched the second unlit lamp off the nightstand, a hard yank pulling the plug free from the wall. Dani clasped it with sweaty fingers.

She faced the door and called herself all kinds of paranoid, especially since she heard nothing. It was probably a drunken guest who'd gotten the wrong room. Or a transient looking for a place to sleep. Or a psycho murdering bastard. All better scenarios than Kelso, who wanted to keep her alive and his prisoner forever.

As nothing happened and no more attempts to open the door were made, she relaxed. The arm holding the lamp dropped. She exhaled.

Then almost choked on a scream as the door was kicked in!

Chapter 6

THE SCENT CAUGHT RORY AS HE BROUGHT DOWN THE cans to the curb. Usually he wasn't the one putting out the garbage, but his cleaning lady had taken the day off due to an unexpected family emergency. Even then, one might wonder why he chose the wee hours to do this particular chore. Surely the morning would have been better suited; however, he'd yet to go to bed, as he'd spent most of the night chasing down false leads online looking for his vanished bride.

All dead ends. Despite having a name and even a face, he couldn't find her. Not a single trace, which led him to being awake at three a.m.-ish, tired, and in no mood to get up in a couple of hours just to put out a few cans.

Setting them on the curb, he paused for a moment. More like his wolf told him to stand still.

What is it?

He didn't get a reply, more of an impression.

I smell something. Someone had been here and left a lingering trace.

He turned his head left and right, looking at the dark shadows, even as he knew he wouldn't see anyone. The scent trail was old. Long gone and decidedly familiar.

Follow it. He didn't question his wolf's demand, his fatigue forgotten as he followed the faint scent trace—and he meant faint. At times he lost it entirely, the soft, elusive fragrance like a misty remembrance. A tendril he would have sworn only he could see.

Twice he almost turned around, thinking he'd finally lost it, but then he'd catch it again. A scuff of the scent along a brick wall. A hint in the air going around the corner.

He told himself that he followed a smell and not a strange tugging that had his feet marching without his direction. And yet, that was a lie.

It was as if an inaudible call directed him, telling him where to go. A strange sensation to be sure and nothing he'd ever experienced before.

He covered the miles between his house and his destination quickly. His pace rapid, his stride long. Soon he stood before a motel that doubtfully ever saw better days. The peachy pink stucco was everything he hated about tourism on the coast. Not his type of place to stay. And none of his friends would either.

Yet, he found himself here. The question being, why? Who did he follow? Had he met them before and forgotten? Perhaps during a drunken binge. A recent Vegas trip came to mind.

A glance at the front office showed it dark. The sign on the door flipped to Closed. The knob not budging, the place locked tight when he yanked.

Yet he didn't turn around and go home. The scent—and that tickling feeling—was stronger here. Whoever he followed had gone into the office and a person only did that for one reason.

He surveyed the darkened block of rooms. Which one had they rented?

And why did he damned well feel like he knew that scent? Who did it belong to? The answer taunted him, teased his wolf, who wouldn't tell him either. His beast simply urged him to keep following.

Despite it looking suspicious, he walked across the front row of the building, sniffing the air by each unit, waiting to get hit by the scent of his prey.

Yes, prey. A wolf didn't follow things out of curiosity like a cat.

Nothing jumped out at him along the bottom floor of the motel. A quick climb up the stairs to the second story and another walk across netted him nothing as well.

He grabbed hold of the railing and leaned on it. Surely the trail didn't just end here. Perhaps the one he followed had gotten into a car and left. In which case, he wasted his time.

Go home. There was nothing here. His wolf had led him on a wild goose chase—except, this time, there was no goose with flying feathers turning around to attack a hungry wolf cub who wanted to bring home some dinner.

The stairs shuddered as he took them down to the

first level two at a time. He hit the parking lot, and he might have kept on going except...the asphalt drive curved around the building. Having never been here before, he didn't know if it was for delivery, more parking, or more rooms.

Go look.

He sighed at his wolf's demands.

You do know we could be at home sleeping in our bed instead of chasing some interesting smell several miles from home.

His wolf didn't say it with words; however, the term "stop bitching, princess" did come to mind, given the disdain his beast oozed.

Knowing he'd never hear the end of it if he didn't, Rory rounded the corner of the motel and was hit by it right away. The scent. Stronger than ever. And not alone. There was something else. Something that shouldn't be here. *Someone in my territory.*

His hackles rose. Now he should note that, technically, this was his father's area—stepdaddy to be correct— as pack alpha for the wolves. But as his son, albeit one who wasn't speaking to him right now, Rory would inherit—once he beat his father in a one-on-one match for dominance.

It was how things worked. One didn't simply inherit a pack. One had to earn it by the might of his teeth and claws.

The fact that he wasn't a natural-born son of the pack leader wouldn't matter. His mother was wolf. It gave Rory every right to rule if he so chose. And, as a wolf, he had a duty to his pack to find out who dared invade their territory without permission.

He didn't need to sniff to notice the door partially ajar, the crack of light from within lighting the edges of it. The splintered jamb let him know not all was right with this scenario. A fact reinforced when the door suddenly swung open and a bulky figure appeared, made even larger by the bundle slung over his shoulder.

Rory took note of the interloper's appearance. Tall, wide, and hairy, his whiskers in need of a good barber. But personal hygiene aside, the large man smelled feline, which naturally caused Rory's lip to curl.

"Who are you?" he barked—with real words and not a woof-woof.

"None of your business, asshole."

"Actually, it is my business. You're on pack land without permission."

"Fuck you and your permission, puppy chow. I've got what I came for. Now get the fuck out of my way, eh?"

A Canadian feline? This got more interesting by the minute, especially when he noted the bundle slung over the other man's shoulder was actually a body wrapped in an ugly comforter. "What have you got there?" Rory asked.

"None of your fucking business, and if you keep yapping at me about it, I'm gonna show you why it's a bad idea to get in my way. Now move."

Rory stood squarely in his path. "As son of the pack leader for this area, I am making this my business."

"You're Beauchamp's son?" The lip curled. "Doubtful, seeing as how he gave my boss permission for me and the boys to conduct our business."

His father had sanctioned a kidnapping? How interesting. "Who is that you're abducting?" Because, despite the blanket wrapped around the shape, something smelled good.

Mine.

His wolf claimed it without seeing it. The last time that happened…

It couldn't be. The coincidence would be too much, but now that the idea had entered his mind and taken root, it wouldn't leave.

"The girl is none of your business," said Cie, short for Canadian Idiot, Eh.

Cie was kidnapping a girl? Ah, fuck. Walk away. Don't look back. Let her handle her own trouble. Don't get involved.

Rory's tarnished inner gentleman polished off his dusty pride and held his ground. "Hand the woman over."

"Like fuck."

Predictable, which meant he had to at least give him fair warning. "Listen, you can either do this the easy way or the hard way. But either way, you are not leaving with the girl."

"You and what army are gonna stop me?" The big fellow made the mistake of thinking he could muscle past Rory. Big guys often mistook his wiry build for weak.

Rory rolled back on his heels, absorbing the blow, before coldcocking the guy.

Crack. It was like hitting granite. He resisted an urge to shake his fist and yell. Because, much like hitting rock, hitting this guy's face fucking hurt.

"You shouldn't have done that." The big cat rolled his free shoulder and dumped his cargo onto the pavement.

Rory backed up a few steps and dropped into a limber partial crouch. He beckoned. "Come on, big boy. Let's see what you've got."

Cie, while a cat shifter in real life, rushed like a bull. Sidestepping was smarter than taking the full brunt. Hence why Rory slid sideways at the last possible moment and stuck out his foot.

The big guy tripped but didn't fall. Rather, he turned with a snarl and came rushing again.

This time, Rory let the fellow barrel into him, and the momentum drove him back into the parking lot, where they hit the hood of a car hard enough to leave a dent.

Oops. Rory and the Canadian cat grappled, exchanging fast blows, blocking others. Dancing to and fro until a particularly well-placed jab staggered Rory. Actually, what made him trip was the damned body in the blanket—which, despite a firm stumble, didn't make a sound.

Is she dead?

He'd have to wait to find out. Cie seemed determined to crush him to death.

"Bear hugs? Is that really your signature move?" he taunted as the man threatened to crack a few ribs. Rory's arms were above the squeeze point, so he clapped his hands over the guy's ears.

The big dude bellowed, and his grip loosened enough for Rory to wedge himself free and push away.

Setting himself in a fighting crouch, he crooked his fingers and beckoned. "Here kitty, kitty."

The man meowed—okay, he bellowed—and came at Rory. They exchanged some blows, most of Rory's landing but doing little damage, while he avoided Cie's plate-sized clenched fists because one of those would probably cause some harm.

The other guy had more than a few pounds on him, and while he lacked skill, he appeared to have a head made of rock. Cie refused to go down.

Which meant Rory would have to play dirty.

When he saw his chance, his foot rose and hit the other guy square in the jewels. Cie predictably *oomphed* and folded. Whereupon Rory grabbed him by the head, yanked him down hard, smashing Cie's face onto his knee. Once, twice, the third time the big guy slumped.

Breathing heavily, Rory stared at the unconscious body on the ground. Good thing there was only one. Or so he assumed.

He frowned at the darkness. There were almost no lights back here. Only shadows upon shadows. Within which anything could hide.

"Gnnnng." The muffled body groaned from the rolled fabric.

What to do with it? Her. *Her...*

He eyed the room spilling light. It took but a moment to enter and get hit by the scent. *Her* scent. He quickly grabbed the bag he found lying there and the few clothes hanging over a chair. She'd not brought much. A quick glance through the bag didn't reveal any keys, or money.

Was this all she had?

Exiting outside, he knew he had to move quickly. At one point, his luck would end and someone would notice two bodies on the ground. He couldn't carry them both home. Not only would that look a bit suspicious, he wasn't strong enough to be hauling around a pair of bodies.

He could have probably handled her, and yet logic reared its head. First, his house was far enough to make it tedious, and two, someone might notice him with his odd burden and ask questions. And three, once big guy regained consciousness, he'd simply follow.

Only if he's alive.

His wolf had very black and white views about the world.

Rory crouched and rifled through the snoring man's pockets. He was rewarded with keys. Rental keys. He aimed them and hit the unlock button.

Lights flashed. Bingo. He now had a set of wheels.

He grabbed the bundled body, brought it to the car, and opened the trunk. Since it didn't have a body already, he gave it one. Then slammed it shut. As for the kitty? Since killing another shapeshifter who had permission to be here might prove problematic, he instead grabbed the heavy man and lugged him into the motel room. He stripped him and tied him to the bed. If found, it would be assumed a sexual act gone awry. It happened more often than people thought.

Shutting the door as best he could, he then got in the driver's side of his newly borrowed car and drove home. Only once in the garage with the door shut behind him did he ponder what to do with the damned vehicle—and the woman in the trunk. The one who smelled so familiar.

It can't be her. No way. The coincidence would be...

Staggering, yes, however, if fate was playing games... He glanced at the bundle form nestled in his trunk. He could find out quite easily. Just peel back that blanket. Free her from the cocoon.

Instead, he threw her over his shoulder and stashed her in his wine storage room—which he kept locked. He didn't have time to deal with her yet and needed somewhere secure to stash her.

Trying to push her out of his mind, he returned to the garage. He still had another problem to deal with.

The car, which had an onboard tracking system—an annoying thing rental companies did to keep track of their fleet—he drove a few blocks to a less-than-nice part of town and abandoned. By dawn, he doubted much of it would remain. A taxi brought him back to his place.

Only once he'd poured himself a glass of whiskey did he debate what to do with the woman he'd found.

He still had no idea who she was.

Liar.

His wolf knew. He suspected he did, too. But, for some reason, he kept avoiding it.

Say it. You're avoiding her.

I don't know for sure it's her. He'd only met and

smelled her that one night. Perhaps this was another woman.

Go look. It was almost a taunt by his wolf.

A taunt he wanted to refuse, but that would indicate cowardice, and Rory's belly was anything but yellow.

He slammed the whiskey glass down and marched to his wine room. Opened the door quickly before he changed his mind then yelled as he was clobbered.

Chapter 7

THE WINE BOTTLE MADE A VERY NICE BONKING sound when it connected with her captor's skull. It unfortunately didn't break. It also didn't send her abductor crashing to the floor. An abductor that looked an awful lot like the man she'd met in the casino. *My husband.*

But how? How had he found her?

"What the fuck?" Rory yelled, holding a hand to the side of his head. "Why are you hitting me?"

Straightening her shoulders, and trying to look tougher than she felt, Dani faced him and tilted her chin. "You kidnapped me."

"No, I rescued you. Or did you conveniently forget the thug I rescued you from?"

She frowned. "What are you talking about? You're the one who kicked in my hotel door and drugged me." She'd not seen his face, but she remembered the fear as the door flung open and hit the wall hard. The strangled scream as the masked intruder entered. The panic when she tried to run, only to find there was nowhere to go, which meant he easily captured her. No amount of flailing freed her. The damp cloth across her mouth, the scent on it acrid, sent her into la-la land.

"That wasn't me, darling. I saved you."

"Really?" She crossed her arms over her chest and arched a brow. "Then explain why I'm locked in this room. Huh? Let's hear it, oh mighty savior."

"I didn't want you escaping until we'd had a chance to talk."

"Talk about what?"

"A certain night in Vegas comes to mind."

Did he know about the wedding? "You know what they say about Vegas."

"It would be easier to forget if we'd not done something a little more binding."

Yup, he knew about the wedding. Her lips pursed. "That was a mistake."

For a moment, she could have sworn annoyance crossed his features before relief smoothed them. "Glad you agree."

"Since that's settled, I'm leaving." Before he touched her and tested her resolve. She might say that night was a mistake, she might be fuzzy on the exact details, but her body hadn't forgotten. Damn her nipples for perking and her pussy for getting slick.

It was toe curling and fun... She blinked and looked away from him lest he recognize the blush on her cheeks for what it was.

"Not too fast, darling. While I'm glad you agree it

was a mistake, there is a certain matter of paperwork to deal with."

"Paperwork?"

"Regarding our marriage."

"Which surely isn't legal. I was drunk."

"No duh. And so was I."

"Aren't there laws, though?"

He shrugged. "I thought we would be covered, but apparently not. Because of what happened after."

"What happened after?" she asked before his arched brow had her cheeks heating. "Oh. That." And by that he obviously alluded to the fact they'd consummated the wedding. "So, we did actually, um..."

"You don't remember?"

She shook her head.

Another long sigh. "Neither can I, but the signs all pointed to it happening."

"And the wedding was real?" She'd seen the name of the chapel. Anything with aliens in it surely couldn't be taken seriously.

"Oh, it's real all right." From his back pocket, he whipped out a folded piece of paper and waved it in her face. "Here's the receipt. There's even a wedding video that I wouldn't recommend watching."

"I can't be married to you." Although, it would solve more than one problem. Kelso came to mind... *Would a marriage keep him away, or would he try and make me a widow?*

"I am glad you agree, which is why I had my lawyer—"

"You contacted someone about it?"

"Well, how the fuck else did you expect me to get a divorce?"

"A divorce?" The word finally filtered through her dense brain. Registering for divorce would involve public filings and an address for the courts. A way to trace her. "No." She shook her head and kept shaking it as she pushed her way past him. "This is bullshit." Her father's favorite expletive slipped past her lips. "This can't be valid. We barely know each other. We can't be married."

"Agreed. Which is why, if you sign this"—he whipped out another set of documents from his magical back pocket—"then we can go about fixing this mess."

"What are those?" she asked, eyeing the tight script with a leery gaze.

"Divorce papers."

"How do you have those already?"

"I had some drawn up the moment I found out about our nuptials."

"Have you been carrying them around all this time?" she asked with a raised brow.

"No, I grabbed them when I found you."

"And locked me up."

"So you wouldn't run away before we took care of business. All we have to do is sign citing irreconcilable differences, then my lawyer files it—"

"Nope." She shoved them back at him.

"What do you mean 'nope'? We can't stay married."

"I agree, which is why we'll both pretend it never happened and go about our lives."

"I'd like to do that, darling, but that means you need to sign the papers." He shoved them back at her.

She tucked her hands behind her back and shook her head. "I can't. Because it has my real name on it."

"You've lost me."

"If I sign that and you file it with the courts, then my real name will be in some database somewhere. Where people can see it." Find it. Find her. She had to leave now.

She began marching in what she hoped was the direction of the front door.

He blocked her.

"Out of my way."

"You are not leaving until you sign."

He didn't appear likely to budge, and it occurred to her that it didn't matter. She would be long gone before anything hit the public waves. "You want me to sign. Fine. I'll sign. But only if you give me a car."

"Like fuck. I saw what happened to the last one you stole."

"I left your car in pristine condition."

"In a bad part of town!"

"You can't blame me for the choices carjackers make." Their mothers should have hugged them more. Her nanny used to give great hugs. Daddy too. Her feet would leave the ground. Her lips turned down.

"Don't you pout. I have every right to blame you for stealing it."

He didn't get to blame her for anything because, "You got me drunk."

"I offered you the first and second. The rest were on you, darling."

"You took advantage of me."

"Did I? Because I most distinctly recall you doing deliciously decadent things to me." His gaze sharpened, something wolfish in his smile.

The man was obviously a rake. Look at how he'd not only conned her into marrying but also into sleeping with him.

"I was drunk, and you took advantage."

He shook his head and jabbed a finger in her direction. "This mess is your fault. You made me marry you."

She might not remember much after the stairwell exit, but she did remember one thing. "Like hell I did. You were the one who said 'Come with me, I've got a surprise.'" The man who called her his mate.

"I was vulnerable."

She snorted. "You? That is the stupidest thing you've said thus far."

"The day is young."

"Is this where I ask what stupid thing you're planning next?"

"No need to ask. Because I'm gonna show you." He lunged suddenly and heaved her over his shoulder.

It took her by surprise, which was why she reacted slowly. Then she did, punching and kicking and yelling.

"Put me down, you big bully."

"That's husband, dear wife."

Sh-i-i-i-t. Did he just seriously say wife? "You can't do this."

"Actually, I can. My house. My rules."

"Abduction is a felony."

"As my spouse, technically, this isn't kidnapping."

"This is abuse," she retorted, even though he'd yet to hurt her. But that would change more than likely if she kept defying him. Kelso had started out nice once upon a time, too. And then she wouldn't give him what he wanted, and things changed. He changed.

Into a cat. But Rory wasn't Kelso.

Yet.

"I haven't hurt you," he said, taking some stairs with ease despite her weight.

"I demand you set me free."

"Will you sign the papers?"

"No." Even if that was why she'd stalked his home. She didn't understand her change of mind. This was what she'd come here for. An escape from this marriage, and now that he offered it—actually, he demanded it—she found herself feeling ornery. This marriage thing could maybe actually work for her.

If her husband wasn't such a misogynistic ass who thought carting women around to get his bullying way was all right.

Rory wanted to control her. Thought he could hold her prisoner and tame her.

Dani was tired of men telling her what to do. Of being stuck in shitty situations.

She lost it.

Chapter 8

I T TOOK R ORY A MOMENT TO REALIZE WHAT THE
sound coming from her was.

Great big heaving sobs.

Holy shit, she's crying.

He quickly set her down on the couch just inside the
guest bedroom and asked, somewhat chagrinned, "Are
you hurt?"

"No-no," she hiccupped.

"Then why are you crying?"

"B-b-because."

He frowned. "Because is not an answer." And why
did he smell fear? "Are you scared of me?"

"Yes."

It bothered him that she might think him capable of
hurting her. "But I wouldn't hurt you."

She sniffled. "You won't let me go."

"No."

"But I want to leave."

Leave? "No!" He might have barked it louder than he'd meant.

She flinched. "You can't control me."

"Never said I was going to. I just want us to talk."

"You mean browbeat until I agree to a divorce."

"Can you blame me?" he retorted. "I'm married to a stranger who took off once, who is trying to take off again, no phone number, no address. You can't seriously think I'd let you disappear without getting this marriage thing handled."

"I really wish I could help you. But, for the moment, I need this marriage. For one, staying out of public records might make it harder for him to find me."

"He? Is someone looking for you?" Jealousy, a new beast, reared its green-eyed head.

"Yeah. So far I've managed to keep ahead of him."

"Are you sure of that?"

"No, why?"

"That guy who broke into your room, the one who actually did try to kidnap you, could he be this fellow you're scared of?"

"What did he look like?" she asked, her fingers twisting in her lap, her cheeks damp with tears.

"About six-foot-three and built like a linebacker."

She shook her head. "Kelso is my height. But it could be one of his thugs."

What kind of coward did that? "And why is this Kelso person sending thugs after you?"

"It's complicated." She averted her gaze.

"I can handle complicated." What he couldn't handle

were those damned tears. He tucked his hands behind his back lest he try and wipe them.

"The less you know, the better. Just like the further away I am, the better it is for you. I shouldn't be here. If Kelso finds out I'm here, you'll be in danger." She went to rise, but he snared her arms and caught her.

She went still, only the fine tremble in her frame and her scent indicating her fear.

"Don't be scared, darling. No one will hurt you while I'm with you." Where did this chivalry come from? And how dare it possess his tongue?

"Hurt me?" She uttered a watery, hysterical giggle. "It's you I'm worried about. You don't know what he is. What he's capable of."

"Actually, I do know, more than you, I imagine." The question was, how much did she know? Because Danita was very human and, as such, probably wasn't privy to the shapeshifter secret.

"You can't know. You couldn't even guess. Because it's crazy. And impossible. Maybe I'm crazy." She pulled her hands free and scrubbed her wet face.

"Let's rewind a bit. Why does this Kelso want you?"

Can't have her. His wolf seemed very adamant on that point. Oddly enough, Rory was in agreement.

"It's—"

"Complicated. So you've said. Explain it anyways."

"Why do you even care? This isn't your problem."

"Because..." He found himself inordinately drawn to her. Because he hated seeing her cry. Because he wanted to kill this Kelso person and then kiss her while saying everything would be all right. Instead, he settled for, "Obviously, you're balking at the divorce because of your problem with this guy. If I help you take care of it, then we can both go singly on our way." The words emerged flat and left a sour taste in his mouth.

Her lips turned down. "I guess."

"Well? What's the deal?"

"It has to do with my father."

Rory might not recall much of that night, but he did remember one fact. "I thought he died."

"He supposedly did. But he didn't leave behind a will. At least not one we could find. I didn't even know he was dead until Kelso appeared one day, knocking at my door looking for it."

"He showed up out of nowhere looking for your father's will?

She nodded.

"Did you know him?"

"Nope. I'd never met him or any of my dad's friends before. He traveled a lot, so when he did come to visit, he spent all of that time with me."

"What of your mother?"

She shrugged. "She died when I was born. I had a live-in nanny until I was nineteen."

The idea of being raised by someone who was paid struck him as lonely. Something in his expression must have shown pity because her lips pursed and her eyes flashed as some of her fighting spirit returned. "It wasn't as awful as it might sound. Elsa took excellent care of me. Her own kids were grown and gone, so she didn't mind acting as a foster mother. She died when I was in college."

"And now your father is gone." Leaving her all alone and vulnerable. "So, what did this Kelso expect to see in your father's will?"

"He wanted to know who inherited from my father. Apparently, Daddy had some investments and stuff. I don't know. Dad never talked business with me. He also never told his business associates he had a daughter. Kelso was rather surprised to meet me."

Which seemed rather odd. Most men proudly displayed their attachments to their children. "I'll bet he was since a daughter would automatically inherit if no will can be found." Understanding dawned. "Did Kelso try to get you to sign over your dad's holdings?"

"No, because he couldn't. As far as the government and lawyers are concerned, my dad is still alive. There's been no formal declaration of his death because there's no body."

"Then—"

"Why did Kelso seem so certain?" A shadow crossed her face. "Because he was apparently there when it happened."

The story sounded very familiar. "We talked about this the night we met, didn't we?" The night he barely recalled. But more and more was wishing he did. Damn that whiskey. He knew better than to mix it with the wine he'd imbibed with dinner. Add the opium smoke and he remembered nothing.

Her lips held a ghost of a smile. "We talked about a

lot of things. I think you thought it was a game given you kept trying to one-up me with your soap opera story of two dads."

"Not a story. It's true. But not the thing we should be concentrating on. This Kelso guy, he's been threatening you?"

She nodded, which only increased the simmering anger within him.

"He's hurt you already."

Again, a nod, which cemented the asshole's fate.

"What's his end game since you can't give him what he wants? Is his plan to kill you and somehow get his hands on your dad's business?"

"Worse." Her lips turned down. "He wants to marry me."

Chapter 9

"Like fuck!" Of all the things to have Rory jump up and exclaim. His eyes blazed and his hands fisted—that was the oddest.

Why would it bother him that Kelso wanted to make her his wife? After all, Rory was bound and determined to ex-wife her as quickly as possible.

"I want you to tell me everything you know about that twatwaffle," he exclaimed, pacing in front of her. She couldn't help but admire him, despite her situation.

Then again, noting how his T-shirt clung to his upper body and how his track pants hung low on his hips was better than remembering her shitty life these past few weeks.

"There's nothing to tell because I don't want you getting involved." The only reason she'd spilled as much as she had was because she'd reached a breaking point. It felt nice to have someone listen to her, to pretend, if only for a moment, she wasn't alone. However, this problem was hers to deal with. Anyone capable of the things Kelso had done wasn't a person she should invite into someone else's life, even if it would be so much easier to not have to handle it herself.

"Too late, darling, because I am already involved."

She flung herself backwards on the bed with a huge sigh. "Why are men so bloody stubborn?"

"I could ask the same of you, darling."

She squeaked as a weight covered her. A manly weight that meant, when she opened her eyes, his face hovered only inches above hers.

"What are you doing?"

"Trying to figure out what it is about you that makes me—"

"Angry?"

He shook his head.

"Stupid?" she asked, since he obviously wasn't too bright, given he kept ignoring her warnings.

His lips quirked. "More like insanely attracted."

Attracted to what? Her? With her tear-stained cheeks, probably blotchy features, and messy hair in dire need of a brush? "You're insane all right." Her lips quirked into a deprecating grin.

"I might go wild on the full moon, but other than that, I'm pretty on the level. Which is why this whole situation with you is aggravating."

"I'm aggravating?" She arched a brow.

"Not in a bad way. It's just I don't know what to think. Since that night, I've been blaming what happened on the booze and opium we inhaled by accident. And yet," he said, his tone musing, "here you are, and once again, I find myself unable to resist." He laced his fingers through hers and tugged them over her head, jolting her already aware body and causing her breath to hitch with arousal. "There is something about you that calls to me."

Odd how he said the things she felt but didn't dare speak aloud. But she did wonder about one thing. "What did you mean that night when you said I was your mate?" The words spilled from her, and her cheeks heated, especially when his eyes widened in surprise.

"I did what?" he asked, only to repeat it more slowly. "Fuck me, I did, didn't I? I called you my mate."

His reaction told her he didn't remember. It caused a pang because she'd not been able to forget. "Drunken ramblings. It happens to us all."

"Was that all it was?" He stared at her intently. A moment fraught with anticipation.

His head dipped. Lower. Lower again.

She held her breath and closed her eyes as his lips pressed against hers.

In this, he was right. Something electric existed between them, and it ignited every time they touched.

It wasn't the booze or the drugs or anything but pure desire.

Her lips parted as his kiss grew demanding, the slant of his mouth over hers coaxing, caressing. The sinuous slide of his tongue brought shivers to her skin. He held her hands still, their fingers laced, and his body, oh the lovely heavy weight of his body, pressed her against the mattress.

The caresses moved from her mouth to follow the line of her jaw. Rather than push him away—because, really, this wasn't the time to be making out—she sighed and arched as he found the lobe of her ear and sucked it. A weakness of hers. His lips then burned a trail down the column of her throat, nipping at her skin, causing her blood to pound furiously and her skin to heat.

His lower body, more specifically his hips, rotated, grinding and applying pressure to her, teasing her. She couldn't help but undulate under him, moving in time with his sensual motions, wanting more. Craving it...

His lips returned to find hers for a torrid kiss, the electrifying sizzle of his touch enough to make her forget why this was probably a bad idea. How could something that felt so good be bad?

He released her hands but only to skim them up her body, sliding them under the fabric of her shirt, his body leaning just enough to the side so he could cup her bra-covered breast. When his thumb brushed over the peak, she uttered a sound that his mouth caught.

But he didn't catch her second moan of pleasure as he bent to capture the tip of her breast, still covered by fabric, with his mouth. He sucked and tugged at her, the barrier between his lips and her skin only adding to the pleasure.

Her fingers threaded through his hair and gripped his head as he toyed with her breast. She gasped when he finally tugged her shirt upwards and out of the way, pushing the cup of her bra aside that he might truly suckle her.

He spent some time teasing that one breast. Took a long moment savoring every inch of her skin and tugging that nipple into an erect point. Then he switched sides and took his leisurely time pleasuring it to the same state while she moaned incoherently.

A part of her tried to warn her—*this is how he convinced me to marry him last time. Seduced me with his skill, made me forget my woes with pleasure.*

She ignored that voice. In his arms, under his caress, she wasn't a pawn in a game, or a victim, but a woman. A woman desired. A woman on the cusp of coming.

His lips trail-blazed a path down her stomach, over her naval to the waistband of her pants. His fingers hooked into the elastic band and began to tug. She'd lifted her hips to help when the phone rang.

More like sang. Something jingled, and he paused.

So did she. "I think someone is calling you," she remarked.

"Ignore it." He certainly appeared intent on doing so as he tugged her pants another inch.

Yet the insistent ringing continued. Stopping only for a moment before starting again.

"Um, Rory."

He sighed. "Yeah. I better answer that, I guess."

"Do you often get calls at"—she glanced over at a clock and frowned—"five a.m.?"

"No, but I kind of expected it. Give me a second, would you?"

A second? He talked as if he'd return and continue, yet the moment he moved away, sanity reasserted itself.

What am I doing?

She sat up on the bed and pulled down her shirt as she heard him answer with a snarled, "Do you have any idea what time it is?"

Time for her to slip out before he returned because, no matter what he said or thought, she wouldn't get him involved.

Couldn't get him involved.

However, her planned escape didn't manage to get very far because her hand had no sooner touched the front door when she heard him say... "And where do you think you're going, wife?"

Chapter 10

I̲t̲ d̲i̲d̲n̲'t̲ s̲u̲r̲p̲r̲i̲s̲e̲ R̲o̲r̲y̲ t̲o̲ s̲e̲e̲ h̲e̲r̲ t̲r̲y̲i̲n̲g̲ t̲o̲ escape, but it did anger him. Only moments before she'd been panting in his arms. Flushed. Beautiful. *Mine.*

And now, without a word of goodbye, she tried to flee.

She whirled and at least had the decently to appear abashed. "I can't stay."

"Considering the trouble my saving you has caused me, I'd have to disagree."

"Trouble?"

"It seems your friend Kelso has connections. Do you know what he's involved in?"

She shook her head. "No. I know nothing." Spoken in a high pitch as she backed into the door.

"You're lying. Tell me what you know of the prick." When she shook her head, he couldn't help but bark, "Now."

Her lower lip trembled, and he felt like a shit, but

then again, after the earful his father gave him, he didn't care. There was something she wasn't telling him. Something that had his father commanding him to hand the girl over. His father might be cutthroat with business, but even he didn't usually cave to pressure. How could he be okay with putting Dani in obvious danger? Rory sure as hell wasn't okay with it.

His answer, "Like fuck," didn't go over well.

"I don't know anything. I swear, I only met Kelso about two months ago when he told me my father was dead."

"And then he kidnapped you, right? Held you prisoner?"

"Because he was trying to convince me to marry him."

"Why not just marry you? Why care if you agreed?"

"That was his plan, except apparently, he has to marry me in front of some family. Seems some of them would have an issue with me showing up gagged. Which was why it became so important I flee."

"You escaped him." And married Rory. *She's my wife.* "You're hitched now, which means he can't force you."

"For the moment, I'm safe. I'll just have to stay far away after the divorce."

Divorce? Logically, he knew that was the next step. But, for some reason, he couldn't help feeling very strongly against it. "No divorce. We're not signing the papers." It made a perverse sense. If she was married, then Kelso couldn't have her.

She can be all mine.

He might have missed a few things as he sat frozen in shock at the idea.

"I don't know what I should do."

"Be my wife." The words emerged again, and this time, he said them with less terror. More firmly.

"It's temping," she mused aloud. "If I'm married, Kelso can't do anything, but at the same time..." She trailed off and looked at him. Her lips turned down, and he wondered at the cause. "I'm not being fair to you."

"How are you not being fair?"

"What of your girlfriend?"

"I'm single. No one to say shit about the fact you're living with me."

"Living? With you?" The expression on her face couldn't have been more appalled. She shook her head. "Give the papers to me. I'll sign."

Except now it was his turn to be ornery. Why did she suddenly want to remove the one barrier keeping her safe?

"Don't be silly."

"It's not silly. You don't know what you're offering. I can't do that to you."

It came to him in that moment. *She's protecting me.*

Ack. The shame of it. His very masculinity demanded that he refuse. "No divorce. I changed my mind."

Her gaze widened. "What do you mean changed your mind?"

"Exactly what it sounds like. I don't want a divorce. I say fuck it, let's make a go of it."

With that stunning announcement, he turned on his heel and headed for the kitchen. It might be too early to start drinking the hard stuff, but a jolt of caffeine wouldn't be amiss.

She followed rather than flee, kind of what he'd hoped when he made his stunning announcement. Made the more stunning because he meant it. He wanted to keep her as his wife.

For now.

Forever.

And that wasn't coming from his wolf. Yeah, there was a bit of that animal instinct, that conviction by his beast that she was *the one*. He also definitely suffered from a case of insta-lust. But there was something else at play here, something exciting and right.

She is the one. And she was trying to get away.

"Get back here and divorce me," she said on his heels.

"No."

"You have to."

"Why?"

"We're not a real couple."

He only turned once he reached the kitchen island. "We could be."

A few blinks of her long lashes occurred before she sputtered, "No we can't. We barely know each other."

"Isn't the getting to know each other bit part of the fun?"

"No."

He kept talking as if she hadn't. "I'm rather enjoying the fact you're cute when angry."

"This isn't funny."

"Never said it was. It's deadly serious, especially since, according to my father, keeping you instead of handing you over might start a war." His douchebag of a father's reasoning as to why Dani had to be given to Kelso. Whereas Rory wondered exactly who the hell Dani was to have a shifter so interested in her. She was one hundred percent human. Did Kelso really only want her for access to her father's business?

Her brow creased. "What does your father have to do with this? What war? And hand me to who?"

"Kelso, of course. Who is coincidentally from Canada. Not the same part my biological father lives in, but close enough for me to wonder why I'm suddenly being plagued by Canadians."

"Well, you don't have to be plagued for long." She marched out of the kitchen, but returned quickly—which was good because he was ready to sprint after her if he heard a door slam shut. She waved the divorce papers at him. "Where's a pen?"

"Coffee?" He offered her a steaming mug, which she ignored to pounce on a jar of pens by the desk area in his kitchen.

She signed with a flourish and slapped the document in front of him. "Done. We are now—"

He grabbed it and tore it into quarters. Then dumped it in the sink, ran some water, and turned on the garbage disposal.

She gaped at him. "Why did you do that?"

"I told you, no divorce."

Out flung her hands. "But that's what you wanted."

"That was before."

"Before what?" she yelled.

Before his father decided to get involved. Yet, even that wasn't the entire reason. One touch. That was all it took to remind him.

She's mine.

Which flew in the face of every bachelor boast and pledge he'd ever made. How his friends would mock him. How the ladies would cry.

Let them lament their loss because, in that moment, he knew one thing for sure. Danita was his mate.

Now he needed to convince her of that.

"So, I was thinking of placing an ad in the local paper."

"An ad for what? A straitjacket?" Ah, there was that delightfully dry humor he enjoyed.

His lips curved. "Don't you mean tuxedo? The ad will be more of an announcement. Mr. and Mrs. Beauchamp recently married in an intimate setting after a whirlwind courtship—"

"Of like a few hours," she grumbled.

"—would like to invite you to a belated wedding reception."

"You want to tell people we're married." Her gaze narrowed. "Why?"

"You said Kelso was determined to wed you. He can't exactly do that if you're already hitched, now can he?"

"You seem to think you're dealing with a normal

person. And I'm telling you Kelso is anything but normal. He'll murder you."

"I'm not that easy to kill."

She made a strangled noise. "Are you not listening? I said he'll murder you. Put a bullet in your head or worse."

"No, he won't."

"The right answer is, 'Holy shit, what do you mean he's willing to kill?' Why aren't you taking this seriously? Don't you get it yet? Kelso doesn't care about laws. He thinks he's above them. He's—he's an animal!"

"So am I." He grinned, but she'd whirled away, her body taut with anger, which was better than the tears. The tears had just about gutted him.

"Again, you're acting like this is some kind of a joke. You don't understand—"

"No, you don't seem to understand." He closed the space between them and grabbed her by the arms, drawing her close. "I don't care who he is or what he wants. Get it through your stubborn skull, I won't let anyone hurt you."

"But—"

He hushed her the only way he knew how, with his mouth. It seemed to work perfectly well given she stopped arguing and kissed him back. While she might argue, she couldn't deny the passion between them.

The fire. Holy fuck, he'd never imagined sharing anything this intense with anyone.

He spanned her waist and lifted her, plopping her ass onto the kitchen island, just the right height for him to insert himself between her legs. She didn't protest. Good thing given how hot he burned for her. His need more than just an ache in his cock and balls. Earlier, he'd seen the mark on her shoulder.

My mark.

He'd not even known he'd done it, but it explained a lot. He'd claimed her. As his mate.

Mine.

It was an old school, piss-on-a-tree kind of way of saying to the shifter world she was off-limits.

And it was a total turn-on. He deepened the kiss, probing her mouth with his tongue, catching all her excited pants and sounds of pleasure. Her fingers dug into the muscles of his shoulders, clinging to him, drawing him closer.

The bedroom interruption had left him simmering with arousal, and he wasn't alone. He could smell her desire. A delicate, mouthwatering perfume that drew him down that he might bury his face between her thighs.

She exclaimed, "Rory!" But didn't shove him away as he blew hotly against the seam of her pants. But that wasn't enough to please him.

He tugged at them, pulling them down and hearing her hiss as her bare cheeks hit the cold granite surface. He made sure to drape her legs over his shoulders and indulged in some sweet honey.

The first lick had him humming, the soft grumbling vibration against her flesh drawing forth a loud moan.

She leaned back, propping herself on her elbows, exposing herself to him. A wanton pleasure for the taking.

He took. He took his time lapping at her sweet nectar. Spent a long moment tugging at her clit until he felt her shivering, on the brink. He shoved two fingers inside her as he knew she grew close, groaning against her sex when her flesh squeezed him tight. He flicked her clit over and over with his tongue as he finger-fucked her, feeling her tighten. Hearing her pants emerge jaggedly amidst mewls of need.

His own cock throbbed, fit to burst inside his pants when she came, her scream long and loud, the ripple of her channel flexing his digits so tight. It was glorious. And, this time, he wouldn't forget.

He stood and reached to draw her close, cupping her head, pulling her to him for a kiss. She had to taste herself on his lips, and yet, she didn't seem to care. She clung to him, her legs locked around his waist. She reached for him, hands pushing at his pants, whispering softly, "Your turn."

The fact that she thought about his pleasure, even though she'd achieved her own, was the only reason why he didn't turn and kill the person who thought they could just walk into his house and bellow, "Boy! Where are you? I know you've got the girl hidden here somewhere. Hand her over right now."

No point in replying. His father would find them quickly enough. While a red-cheeked Danita quickly straightened her clothes, he turned and shielded her with his body, ready to confront his father, who stormed into the kitchen.

"There you are! What the fuck do you think you're doing? Trying to start a war?"

Arms crossed, Rory regarded his father, a big and swarthy man who looked nothing like him. Yet, in temperament, they were often alike.

"Most people knock and wait to be invited before just barging in and interrupting."

"Interrupting?" Dark brows, only hinting at gray, rose high over piercing eyes. A gaze that quickly took note of Rory's disheveled appearance, the woman behind him, and the lingering scent of pussy—the edible kind—in the air. "For fuck's sake, boy. Is that why you took the girl? So you could fuck? You do know she's engaged to someone else."

"Not anymore she isn't."

"Are you insane? Are you doing this to get back at me?"

"What makes you think this is a revenge plot? And since when do you jump to obey anyone else?"

"I am not jumping," his father declared. "Merely averting some unpleasantness. You took someone you shouldn't have."

"That douche bag stole her first against her will."

"That's not what he's claiming."

"He's lying," she exclaimed.

His father's laser stare tried to burn her. "Stay out of it. You've caused quite enough trouble already."

"Don't talk to her like that." Rory bristled. "You will speak to her with respect or get the fuck out of my house."

"Excuse me?" The incredulity in his father's voice might have been funnier, except it probably meant the temper was close behind. "You don't get to speak to me like that. Ever. I'm—"

"Not my father."

That darkened the look. "Perhaps not by blood, but I raised you. I promised your mother to treat you as my son."

"And I'm telling you that you don't have to anymore."

"You're a Beauchamp, like it or not, and you're also a member of *my* pack. Mine. Which means, as your alpha, you obey me."

"Watch what you say." Rory inclined his head, indicating Danita.

For a moment, he thought his father would explode, especially since his father had almost spilled some secrets. Secrets he wasn't yet sure Danita was privy to, despite the felines after her.

"You should know better than to get involved in the business of others."

Rory patted Danita's knee. "But she is my business." And then, before his father could say another word, he announced it so there would be no misunderstanding. "I'd like you to meet my wife."

Chapter 11

DANI COULD STILL HEAR THE ARGUING FROM upstairs. When given the chance—in the form of one steely-eyed daddy glaring at her and saying, much too politely, "Would you mind if I spoke to my son alone?"— she fled. Not out the front door, even if it tempted, but upstairs.

She retraced her steps to the bedroom and paced.

What is going on?

An odd situation had gotten stranger. Mostly because Rory's dad knew about Kelso. Knew he was looking for her and wanted to hand her over.

Just who were these people?

Mob? Most likely, even if Rory didn't seem the type. How else to explain this talk of packs and alliances? Not to mention the kidnapping and violence, at least on Kelso's part, but even Rory didn't seem fazed one bit by it.

Is he a gangster, too? An upper-echelon one, obviously, given his standard of living. *Dear God, am I married to the mob?*

Wasn't that a movie? She seemed to recall having watched something along those lines. It never ended well for the wives.

And here I am sticking around like a ninny.

Except where else could she go? Her attempt to escape had failed. Add to that she now found herself married, without money or resources. It was enough to bring back the tears, especially as the arguing stopped and a door slammed.

A moment later, Rory stood in the doorway, a forbidding man with a rigid jaw. Probably because he was about to toss her out on the street or hand her over like his father wanted.

She couldn't blame him. Nobody wanted the trouble she brought.

"I guess I should pack my things." Not that she'd really unpacked. Her bag still sat on the floor where it had gotten tossed.

"Probably a good idea."

He folded his arms and watched as she stuffed the dirty clothes—dirty and smelling of sex—and then put the flap over the top.

As she approached him, he held out his hand for it.

"I can carry it."

"If you insist. This way." He held out his hands and swept her out, and only a few steps later did she realize he'd moved away from the stairs. "Where are we going?" Was there a rear entrance to this place?

"Your new bedroom," he said, nudging her toward a bigger doorway, the dual doors open and leading into—

"This is your room," she exclaimed, whirling on him.

"Our room," he corrected.

"But I thought..."

"That I was going to obey my father and just hand you over?" He shook his head and smiled. "Like fuck." Not exactly a romantic declaration, and yet it warmed something cold inside her. "We're married, darling."

"By accident."

"I prefer to call it fate."

"Fate?" She snorted. "I've never heard booze and drugs called that before."

"Fate moves in mysterious ways."

"You're just doing this to piss off your father." Rebellion was a thing she knew. She'd gone through a period of it in her teens when she got tired of her father's sporadic visits.

"No, that's just a bonus. Being married to you, I have a feeling," he said, advancing on her, "will have its own bonus."

"Better enjoy it while you can. You might not live long," she muttered.

"There you go casting aspersions on my ability to survive. I am stronger than you think."

Perhaps, if faced with other humans, but Kelso would eat him alive. Literally. But she couldn't exactly tell him that. He'd think she was nuts. And maybe she was. Perhaps her mind had turned Kelso into some kind of werecat-like monster rather than deal with what she'd endured. This wouldn't be the first time she'd imagined giant cats in her life. She still remembered as a child coming down to the kitchen for a glass of water, half asleep, and yet waking really quickly when she saw the lion curled up in front of the gas fireplace.

The sound of shattering glass was hidden by her screams as her little feet pounded up the stairs screaming for her nanny. Only it was her daddy who came racing to find her, shirtless and disheveled, grabbing her in his arms and soothing her. Telling her it was just a dream.

Arms circled around her again in the here and now. Big arms. Strong arms. While they offered a certain comforting security, they also aroused. Everything about Rory Beauchamp ignited her. It made her weak, too. Utterly damsel-like weak. She relaxed into his hug and leaned her head against his shoulder.

"I wish my life was simple."

"Probably not going to happen, darling, but you don't have to be alone anymore."

And perhaps that was the best thing she could hope for.

She clung to that, just like she clung to him later in the shower he insisted on sharing. A shower that involved his soapy hands on her body, skimming over her curves.

His fingers brushed the crescent moon of the bite mark he'd given her during their first encounter. He kissed it, and she forgave him the faint scar. Especially once she saw the nail marks she'd left on his back after he took her hard against the shower wall.

She loved it. Loved how his cock sank into her deep,

filling her, stretching. The climax he'd given with his fingers and tongue was nothing compared to the rippling ecstasy of coming on his shaft.

It was only once her legs unwound from his waist and she rinsed herself—for the second time—that she realized they'd used no protection. Which was cause for concern, especially since Kelso had taken away her birth control pills. Preparing her, he said, for when she came crawling.

Surely the effects of the pills would linger for a bit? Right? She chose not to dwell on what would happen if they didn't. Just like she chose to ignore her queasy stomach the following morning.

She blamed it on the way he nonchalantly told her what he'd planned for the evening. "The announcement of our wedding went out in the paper this morning." He slid his phone across the table to show her the printed notice.

It didn't help her nausea.

"You put the address for the reception in the ad," she noted.

"Might as well. It's not as if we were keeping it a secret."

"Kelso might show up with his men."

"I should hope so since this is for his benefit."

She tossed him a sharp look. "You're baiting him."

"Yes."

"After everything I told you?"

"Yes."

She stared at him, his freshly washed and combed hair. His beard, neatly trimmed. His nonchalance as he pounded back more food than a man that trim should eat. "Who are you?"

"Your husband."

"I mean, who are you? What do you do for work?"

"I'm a dealer of sweets."

"You sell drugs!"

He looked startled. "While our candy might be considered addictive, in our defense, so are chips and other delicious foods."

She stared at him blankly.

A smile stretched his lips. "I'm part owner of Lip Smackn' Syrup and Candy. It's a family-owned business that produces all kinds of sweet goods from candy to syrup."

"You're a candy maker."

"Yes."

"Which is a front for your mob activities?"

"My what?" He laughed. A boisterous and loud sound. "You think we're mob?"

"Your dad said you betrayed the pack."

"Which, in my world, is another word for family. You're pack now." He nuzzled her, inhaling her scent as he so often did. Strange, but comforting at the same time, even if his mannerisms reminded her of her friend Sarah and her dog.

Dani never owned a pet as a child. Father used to curl his lip at canines, and the one stray cat she'd adopted got one look at her dad on a visit and disappeared. She stuck to virtual pets after that devastating event.

"Do we have to throw this party?" she said with a sigh.

"Yes. And not just because I want to make it clear to my father and Kelso this marriage is real." Which it wasn't, no matter how many times he pretended. But, for the moment, she could pretend, too, and bask in the comfort. "I want everyone to know you're my mate."

"Your mate," she repeated with a wrinkle of her nose. "You make it sound like you own me."

"Would you feel better if I said I was your mate?"

It had a nice ring, but still. "How about we crawl back into bed and hide instead?"

He liked that idea. Although there was little crawling done. Lots of heavy breathing and sweating, yes. But that didn't save her from the evening's event being held at a fancy restaurant he'd reserved.

He'd even arranged a lovely dress, as well as various toiletries, including makeup and perfume. The crowning touch being the jewelry he insisted on bestowing upon her. She shivered as he placed the necklace around her neck, the fine chain light. The pendant hanging from it in the shape of a moon inset with opals glistened every time it caught the light.

All the preparation didn't quell the butterflies in her stomach. She felt like an intruder, a fraud. These people, his friends, family—and possibly her enemies—had gathered to celebrate a drunken mistake. His change of heart, and so quickly, made no sense to her.

He'd gone from demanding divorce to refusing to trying to convince her they should make a go of it.

Which was crazy. What did they have in common other than chemistry?

Then again, wasn't that how all relationships started? She'd asked her father once how he and her mother had met. Depending on his mood, they'd met through mutual friends at a party. And yet, more than once, when drunk, on the anniversary of her death, he'd alluded to something a little more exotic, saying he'd laid claim to her the moment he'd seen her.

Because, oddly enough, her big and burly father, with his golden hair and bushy beard, believed in love at first sight.

Danita, on the other hand, was more pragmatic. Surely there was more to love than liking someone's look —or how they kissed in bed. Or did she delude herself?

One thing was certain, none of the boys in her teens, and then men in her twenties, ever evoked the strong reaction Rory did by just looking at her. None ever made her knees weak when he touched her. Only Rory could make her panties wet when whispering against her lobe, "I can't wait to peel that dress off you later."

"I say we do that now," was her mumbled reply as they entered the restaurant and became the focus of too many eyes.

Instead, he lifted their clasped hands and drew the crowd's attention. They quieted, and in that silence, he firmly declared, "My wife, Danita Beauchamp." Just about everyone in the place clapped and whistled. Some even howled, which was a little unnerving.

Only one small group by the bar didn't react in a

positive manner, and Dani clung closer to Rory as she spotted Kelso and his crew.

The nausea was back in her belly, crawling up her throat.

"I take it that's the guy," Rory said with a slight tilt of his head.

She could only give a short bob.

The fool man tugged her toward Kelso rather than away. She almost dug in her heels, and yet how would that look?

She did her best to hide her trembling as they approached Kelso and his posse.

He can't hurt me here. Not in front of a crowd. Brave words. She just hoped they were true.

"So you must be the douche nozzle that thinks it's all right to terrorize women."

Dani could have groaned at Rory's taunting words.

"And you're the idiot dog who wants to start a war over sloppy seconds."

At that, Dani winced, but also found a spurt of anger enough to say, "I never slept with you."

"Is that what you told the dog? And he believed it? Did she tell you we spent weeks at my cottage? Together. All alone. Not much to do in the woods in the fall other than lounge in bed." Kelso winked, and while some women might have found him attractive, she sure as hell didn't. He wore his hair like an eighties rock star: dirty blond, longer in the back, but not quite a mullet. He was clean shaven and wearing an open-necked shirt.

His looks didn't impress her. Neither did his claim

they'd slept together. Indignation drew her ramrod straight. "We did not have sex!"

"I don't know why you're lying about it. I just wish I'd known you were dying to get married. Especially given your condition."

"My condition?" She regarded Kelso with puzzlement. What was his game? Why did he lie about what had happened?

"I'm surprised puppy chow over here can't smell it himself. Let me ask you, have you been feeling queasy lately?"

As a matter of fact, she felt queasy right about now, especially as Kelso kept talking and Rory's face turned into a frozen mask.

"...understand now why you had to get married so quick, given your baby needs a daddy."

Baby?

"You're pregnant?" Rory sounded shocked, but not as much as her. Enough that she fainted for the first time in her life.

Chapter 12

THE ANNOUNCEMENT HIT HER LIKE A GHOSTLY LEFT hook, and she went down hard.

Rory caught Danita before she hit the floor.

She wasn't faking it. Not the fainting and, now that he was looking for it, not her scent. What did shock him was the fact he'd not caught on to it sooner. Then again, he'd been so overcome with rutting lust he'd not smelled much other than their mutual desire.

But if he took a moment, and really allowed himself a good sniff, then it wasn't hard to find it, that ripeness of a womb quickening. With child.

Supposedly another man's child.

Was that the reason why she'd married him in Vegas and then refused initially to divorce him? Had she planned to pass off the child as his?

"I can see you're a little shocked, puppy chow. Understandable. She's been a flighty thing since her father died. Needs a firm hand, this one. I know how to handle her, so tell you what. I'm gonna make it real easy for you. I won't cause trouble for you and your pack so long as you divorce her and let her leave with me."

Leave? Rory frowned. How could he let Danita go with a man who so obviously terrified her? How could he let her leave with any man period?

"She's not going anywhere." Not until he'd had a chance to figure shit out. He didn't want to act hasty. Last time he'd acted first, he'd gotten fucked. This time...he needed to be careful.

For the moment, he was stunned. He'd only just begun to wrap his head around the idea he was married— and not minding it. To find out she carried a child— whose child?—put a whole new spin on things.

What if Kelso lied? What if it was his baby she carried? He stared at her still flat stomach.

Mine.

He swept her into his arms, ignoring the hushed murmurs around him. Too many had witnessed what happened and, given most everyone in the restaurant was a shifter, probably heard the words exchanged. Still, a man should always hold his head high.

Rory cleared his throat. "If you'll excuse me. It would seem my blushing bride is overcome with all the excitement." He exited the main dining area and then outside again to his parked car. He gently placed her on the backseat and had just closed the door when he heard footsteps.

Whirling, he unclenched his fists as he noted Connor, his lawyer and friend. "Did you just arrive?"

"In time for the floorshow. So this is the woman you want to divorce." Connor bent down to peer through the window. "I can see why. Cute face, still, though, sounds like she comes with lots of baggage."

"Understatement," Rory said with a sigh. "Want to hear a crazy thing, though? We were actually planning to make a go of it."

"Were? I take it you changed your mind."

Rory scrubbed a hand over his face. "I don't know what I want to do anymore. You heard what happened in there. That bastard is claiming she's carrying his baby."

"Is she?"

"I don't know. What I do know is if she is..."

"Then what?"

"Then is it fair for me to take it away from its real daddy?" And then, because Connor knew the truth, he continued. "I mean, that's what my mother did. Passed me off as a true Beauchamp. Kept me from my real dad."

"But you still had a dad."

A tough old wolf who raised his only son sternly. Who barked more often than he wagged. "Yeah, but how different would my life be if I'd known the truth? And here I am, stuck in a similar situation, married to a woman carrying another man's kid." Because surely it wasn't his. It was too soon. "Maybe I should let her go with Kelso." The moment he said it, he knew he couldn't do it. Just fucking couldn't, which pulled a sound from him as he pushed away from the car.

"What does she want to do?" Connor asked.

Perhaps the thing they should all be asking. "She

doesn't want to be married to douche nozzle, that's for sure. And the only thing protecting her is marriage with me." Married because of circumstance and not because she wanted to be hitched to him.

Someone signaled from the restaurant. His mother. The one person he couldn't ignore. He glanced back at the car and his unconscious wife. He shouldn't leave her.

Connor saw him and shook his head. "Lock the doors. She's not going anywhere."

"Kelso's here."

"He'd be a fucking moron to break into your car and steal her."

True. Then again... "It might be easier if she was gone before I came back." He immediately regretted saying it. "We better go say hi and tell people what's going on." He turned to look back at the car as he walked away, the sensation of wrongness strong, and yet Connor was right. He couldn't ignore his mother, nor could he exactly carry Danita around like a limp doll.

Connor kept pace with him as he returned to the restaurant. "No one will blame you if you divorce."

Divorce? That seemed a little hasty. His feelings for her might be in a state of chaos, but the core of them remained. She was his mate. "What will people say if I don't divorce?" He stopped before the restaurant door and whirled. "What if I said I can't stand the thought of her being with another man? That I don't care if she's carrying another man's baby?"

"I'd say it's your life, your choice." Connor shrugged. "Do what makes you happy."

"What would make me happy is punching that smug cat in the face."

"Would you like me to hunt him down?"

Yeah, he kind of would. But first, he had to deal with his mother, who insisted on introducing him to someone. All the while he could think only of Dani. Who was alone.

What if she woke and ran?

What if Kelso still wanted her?

Even though he'd been gone only minutes, it felt like longer, especially with his inner beast pacing. He made his excuses and headed outside. The car was locked, in a well-lit area with lots of traffic. No one would have done anything to her.

Yet he wasn't surprised to discover the backseat empty. Danita was gone. The question was, did she leave of her own volition or had someone taken her?

Chapter 13

Dani's lashes fluttered, but she didn't move or open them as she listened in and heard Rory's words.

"It might be easier if she was gone before I came back."

She couldn't blame him. Rory didn't believe the baby was his, and Kelso's lies were believable. Yet, the fact that Rory chose to believe him over her hurt. When he walked away, she sat up, lower lip trembling.

Here came the pity party. The same one she'd suffered from when her daddy would leave on one of his long absences and she felt all alone in the world. Abandoned.

Why is it I can't keep anyone close?

Why couldn't she find someone to love?

Sniffle.

Well, one thing was for sure, she wasn't about to stick around for the excuses and the dumping. Rory obviously didn't want her.

But the baby is his.

And maybe once the baby was born, she'd return to prove it. To shove the fact in his face.

However, she had about eight months before that would work. Eight months to find a new place to hide.

She exited the car and stood, looking around at her options. No car keys meant no stealing his wheels. Pity, they were nice, almost as nice as the last car of his she'd boosted.

With nothing on her but a fancy dress, heels, and jewelry, she began to walk, her gaze intent on the sidewalk and street. If she could find a pawnshop, surely she could get something for the earrings he'd given her.

Or you could finally give Daddy's lawyer a call. He had promised to help her if she needed it. Except she wasn't quite sure she trusted him. Something in his eyes. The way he moved. The fact that he asked her, "Would marrying Kelso be so bad?" Making her wonder if he really had her best interests at heart.

The clack of her heels moving away from the restaurant toward the road sounded loud even over the noise of the cars prowling the street. Perhaps that was why she didn't hear the approach of someone behind her.

Someone who placed a heavy hand on her shoulder. Who said, "Are you Danita?"

She whirled and beheld an older gent with whitish-silver hair, his topcoat buttoned, a scarf at his neck. "Who are you?" she asked.

"If you are Danita, then I am a friend of your father's. I was sent to find you."

"Who sent you?" He mentioned the name of her father's lawyer. Her eyes widened.

"Why did he send you?"

"Because he thinks you're in trouble."

Understatement. Still, though, given her troubles of late, she wasn't as quick to trust. "How do I know you're telling the truth?"

"Would it help to mention I knew your mother? You are the spitting image of Rebecca Jean."

The fact that he knew that was enough for her to dive into the luxurious comfort of a car. The door slammed shut behind the stranger, and he leaned forward and said, "Airport. And lose any tails."

Then he leaned back, his Old Spice cologne a comforting scent that reminded her of Daddy.

"Who are you?" she asked. "How come we've never met before?"

"Because your father always kept his family life separate from everyone else. And we'll talk about that. But first, is it true you're pregnant?"

In reply, her stomach gave a lurch, and she spilled its contents on the man's lap.

Chapter 14

Discovering Danita was gone did something to Rory. It ignited his anger. *Goddammit, she ran again.* Quickly followed by fear. *What if she didn't?* Kelso seemed pretty intent on getting his claws on her. Because he thought the baby was his. But what if...what if he lied? What if, as she claimed, he'd never touched her?

Nothing Rory recalled of that first night with her spoke of any prior claim. She bore no scent. No mark. She did, however, after their night together.

Bloody hell, that bastard lied.

Rory stormed back into the restaurant and ran into his father. Just the man he wanted to see. "Where is that bastard cat staying?"

"Are you talking about Kelso Pumeaux and his pride?"

Rory's lip pulled back in a sneer. "Lions have prides. He's just an alley cat who took something of mine."

"You mean the girl? He technically had prior claim."

Rory jabbed a finger into his chest. "Like fuck. She's my wife. She bears my mark. Not his."

"According to him, she's bearing his child."

"He's lying."

"Why would a man lie about something like that?"

"You did. You told the world I was yours."

His father's lips tightened. "To save your mother the humiliation."

"Don't you mean to save your own pride? How would it look if it was known the mighty leader of the pack had his wife step out on him?"

"We were having troubles."

"I'll say. She fell for another man." A man who'd left her and returned to his own wife.

"We were in a tough position in our marriage. We got past that."

"Yeah, you got past it so well you've been a dick to her."

"At times our relationship is strained."

"Understatement. And not the point."

"I'd say it is. You look at me and blame me for being a dick to you and your mother. Well, think of it from my view. The woman I loved, my wife, cheated on me. She didn't just sleep with another man, she fell in love with him. Got pregnant by him. He gave her the one thing I couldn't. Exactly how should that make me feel?"

The restaurant at their back got quiet, too quiet, as the drama played out. His father dragged him outside. But Rory wasn't done.

"If you were so mad, then why not divorce her?"

"Because I loved her, dammit. Even though she betrayed me. I love your damned mother. And because I couldn't let her go, I did my best to forgive, to move past that, to accept you as my son."

"But a part of you hates me."

At those words, his father's expression softened. "Is that what you really think?"

"You were hard on me my whole life."

"Because I wanted you to succeed. I tried too hard to be the man I thought you needed."

"A cold fish?"

"Not cold, afraid." His mother emerged from the restaurant and placed a hand on his father's arm. "Your father loves me, and I betrayed him." Before Rory could jump to her defense, she shook her head. "I did. We were struggling with the fact he couldn't give me a child. And I was weak. I turned to another man for comfort."

"A man who abandoned you."

"A man who returned to his family, just like I returned to your father. I can't say I wish I'd done things differently because, otherwise, I wouldn't have you."

"A constant reminder," he said bitterly.

"Yes, a reminder to your father that, if he gets too close, one day, you might betray him, too. Leave him for another man. Call someone else father."

The reasoning struck Rory, and he physically reeled. "Do you really think I'd abandon you?"

His father shrugged. "The first thing you did when you found out was run to find him."

"Because I was curious." And, yes, angry. Angry his parents kept it all a big secret. "But I came back."

"I know. Thank you."

Surprise made Rory blink. "For what?"

"For coming back. For still calling me father. For—"

Before the man could spill another word, Rory threw himself at him, giving him a rare hug that was returned amidst applause from those who emerged to watch—and probably craved popcorn.

Mother inserted herself in the middle, and they shared a rare moment of family togetherness that ended with his father's gruff, "About the girl..."

"My wife."

"Raising another man's child is hard."

Yeah, but his dad had done it. "I don't care." Danita was his mate.

"Very well. Here's where he's staying."

Rory didn't wait for reinforcements. Although he didn't eschew Connor's aid—given he didn't have a choice, as his friend hopped into the front seat of the car.

The hotel the cats were staying at was one Rory knew, which meant getting to the penthouse level was easy. Kicking in the door somewhat satisfying. Not scenting Danita at all, worrisome. But his true pleasure came when Kelso rose from the couch and exclaimed, "What the fuck are you doing here?"

"Where is she?"

The other man's lip curled. "Did you lose your new bride already?"

"I know you took her. Where is she?"

Kelso raised his hands. "Not here, and not with my men. I guess she ran away. She has a habit of doing that."

Rory stalked closer, every inch of him bristling. "If you harm a single hair on her head..."

"You'll what?" the other man taunted. "Start a war? Go ahead. I'm the leader of the Canadian pride now. Which means I'm allied with my American cousins. Is the pack really ready to go to war over a woman?"

Rory wanted to scream "yes." Except Connor placed a hand on his arm, the voice of reason and caution. "She's not here, dude."

He knew that. Sensed it even. Yet that did nothing to quell his rage. The man in front of him had hurt her. Terrorized her. His wolf demanded justice.

Instead, he had to content himself with a threat. "Stay away from Danita."

"Or else what, puppy chow?"

"Or I will start a war."

Chapter 15

Dani was on a plane back to Canada of all places, with a man she'd never met before but who claimed to be Rory's real daddy.

"So let me see if I have this straight. You used to go to school with my dad. You knew my mom. Plus, you're Theo Elanroux, Rory's biological father." A twist she'd not expected. "But Rory won't talk to you. At all."

"Correct."

"And yet, Rory's other daddy, the one who raised him, invited you to our wedding reception."

"Yes."

"Why?"

"According to him, he wanted to mend fences. To right a wrong."

Remembering the man she'd met, she found that hard to believe. Her skepticism showed.

Theo spread his hands. "I know, I was shocked too,

but apparently, it is possible for a man, even Jack, to feel regret."

"I still don't get your interest in me. Rory doesn't want me anymore."

"He'll come around. Especially once he realizes you carry his child."

"I haven't even taken a pregnancy test yet. How come you're all so certain?"

Theo tapped his nose. "It never lies."

There they went with the whole smell thing again.

She cocked her head. "What makes you so sure it's his? He seems to think it's Kelso's."

At that, Theo snorted. "Your scent is all wrong. You carry my grandchild."

"I guess." She folded her hands over her still flat stomach. "If you want, I can make sure you get visitation once he or she is born."

"Rory will come around before then."

"I doubt it. Rory never really wanted to get married in the first place."

"But let me guess, once you met, he couldn't help himself."

She snorted. "We were drunk."

"However, I will wager, when you met again, this time without the influence of alcohol, was the attraction still there?"

Her cheeks heated. "I'd rather not discuss this."

"Very well, let me ask you, once my son met you, did he still want the divorce?"

"He did at first."

"But changed his mind."

Curiosity had her querying, "How do you know that?"

"Because you bear his mark."

"This ring?" She held up her hand. "He just put it on me today." She twisted it off, a heavy lump of metal and stone that meant nothing. "It was all for show at the fake reception party."

"Fake? Oh, my dear, you have much to learn."

"Is this where you claim you're going to teach me?" She managed to hold in a snort. Many of this old man's mannerisms were kind of funny. However, he did provide a way out of a sticky scenario, and a free flight back to Canada. Since running hadn't worked, she'd need a new plan.

"I already taught one grandson what it meant to be an Elanroux. I am sure I can do it again."

"You keep assuming I'm going to stay with you."

"Probably not for long. I imagine once Rory realizes where you are, he'll come for you."

"Doubtful." She could still hear his hurtful words.

Theo reached forward and patted her knee. "Don't be so certain about that. You underestimate your allure."

"I'd prefer less allure. Ever since my daddy disappeared, it's been a non-stop nightmare. I still can't believe you knew my daddy."

"Knew?"

Her lips turned down. "Daddy is dead."

"Your father?" He frowned. "Are you sure of that?"

She nodded.

"We are talking about Gregory Leopold? Big man, blond hair, early fifties but looks much younger?"

"Yes. He died about two months ago."

Theo's lips flattened. "I'd heard rumors, but thought they were just that, rumors."

"It's true."

"How certain are you of his death?"

Remembering Kelso's taunting laughter and cruel admission, she said, "Pretty sure."

"I can't believe he didn't better protect you." Theo shook his head, his words cryptic. Just what was her father involved in? "Well, you needn't worry any longer. Staying with me will keep you safe from those like Kelso wanting to take advantage. At least until Rory arrives."

"Rory's not coming."

"He will once I call him."

She shook her head. "You are not calling him."

"But—"

"No."

"He's your husband."

"If you really want to help me, then you'll help me find a lawyer and get the paperwork started on a divorce."

Theo's mouth twisted. "Rory won't allow it."

"Give it a few weeks." That was all it would take for him to forget.

Chapter 16

IF ONLY HE COULD FORGET.

But he couldn't.

Even as Rory searched and failed to find Danita, the memory of her plagued him. It was if she'd vanished that night at the restaurant. Rory couldn't find a trace of her, and yet he searched. Commercial airlines. Buses. Trains. Hell, he even had a friend in law enforcement run vehicles stolen the night she disappeared.

However, someone had covered her tracks well. Monitoring Kelso and his crew proved futile. Either he was pretending to not know her location or he was also at a loss. Rory's men reported back that Kelso seemed to be hunting Danita, too. Kelso stuck around for two weeks before he headed back home.

Without Danita.

The only good thing to come out of the mess was an improved relationship with his father. Yes, father and not stepdad. That was disrespectful of the man who'd raised him, and now that Rory had gotten past his anger, he saw that.

He also realized that Elanroux wasn't to blame for everything either. Without him, Rory would have never been born. Seemed kind of dumb to hate the fact of his conception. It also seemed stupid to hate a man who never got a chance to be a father.

Which was why Rory finally called his bio dad's number almost a month after Danita vanished into thin air.

The old man answered, a tad too eagerly. "Rory, son, I am delighted to hear from you."

"Don't call me son." Holding out a hand didn't mean he was ready for a mushy kind of relationship.

"As you wish. To what do I owe the pleasure?"

"Um..." All the words he'd practiced fled. His usual brash nature hid. What exactly did one say to the man whose life he'd barged into with fiery consequence?

"Would you like to meet and talk?"

Yes. Rory wanted to know more about the man whose genetics ran in his blood. "Meet? Um. Not yet. I was just calling to..." say he wanted to start over. That he'd like to get to know him. That... "I like your new company commercial."

In an odd twist of fate, his fathers owned highly competitive businesses. His bio dad dabbled in the organic maple syrup business while his father worked with synthetic sugar.

"You didn't call to talk about a dancing bottle of syrup."

"No." He sighed. "Listen, I called because—"

"Theo, what do you want for dinner? Cook is not feeling well today, so I'm going to attempt to cook. I can make tacos or grilled cheese, usually without burning them."

Rory heard *her* voice and froze. "Who is that?" he asked.

"My, uh, nurse." Elanroux coughed. "I've been feeling a little under the weather." Hack. Cough. "Let me call you back."

Click.

Rory stared at the phone.

You've got to be kidding me. Here he was calling his bio dad to mend fences and the bastard was the one hiding Danita this entire time.

Fucker!

He fired off a text to Connor. *Take a few days off.*

Why?

Because he was going back to Canada to fetch his secret Vegas bride.

Chapter 17

SHE AWOKE WITH THE STRANGEST SENSATION OF being watched. Which was highly unlikely. She'd seen how seriously Theo took his home security, especially once he knew of the danger to her. No one could get into his house without permission.

Still, the feeling of someone staring wouldn't stop. She sat up, the pitch-black room silent, and yet she could have sworn she smelled something. Musky and masculine.

Familiar.

Impossible.

She leaned over to slap at the lamp, the touch pad reacting immediately. It emitted a soft glow, enough to see who sat in a chair across from the bed.

She gasped. "Rory, what are you doing here?" She couldn't help but stare at him, drinking in the sight. He would look just as yummy as she remembered. Angrier, too.

"Why do you think I'm here? To bring you home, of course."

The statement startled her. "That's not my home."

"If you don't like the décor, then change it."

"It's not the house that's the problem." She hugged her upper body. "I know you don't want me."

"You couldn't be more wrong." His eyes flashed, almost yellow in the murky shadows beyond the pool of light. Something inside her shivered. "You're my wife, and I want you to come home with me."

"I already have a home." A home she'd feared returning to because of Kelso.

"Your only place is with me." He made as if to lunge from the chair.

"This is crazy." She tucked the blanket tighter. "We should be getting a divorce."

"Not happening, darling."

"I'm still pregnant." She stated it boldly. Chin raised.

"All the more reason to return with me. Our child is going to have two parents."

"Our?" Her brow arched. "I know you don't think it's yours."

"Maybe it is, and maybe it isn't. You want to know what I realized that night you left?" He stared at her, intent and serious. "It doesn't matter who donated the sperm. If my dad could raise me to be the man I am, then I can do no less."

"I don't understand. Why do this? Why are you so determined to have me? You could have any woman you wanted."

"Yet all I want is you."

The words melted any resistance she might have had. She held open her arms, and he was in them, holding her close. Kissing her.

And she was kissing him back. The electrical awareness as strong as ever. Their passion too intense for much foreplay.

"I've missed you so much," he groaned, skimming up her nightgown.

"I missed you more." She sighed as he penetrated her, the thick length of his shaft filling her right.

"I won't lose you again. I'll microchip you if I have to," he grunted as he built a rhythm.

"Don't leave me," she asked softly as she wrapped her limbs around him.

"Never. You're mine. *Mine.*"

He growled the word as he came, and she raked his back as she joined him, their bodies frozen in a tense moment of intense pleasure.

He held her cradled in his arms, careful to not crush her with his weight. "I missed you," he stated.

"You barely know me."

"Yet, we connected enough that you left a hole behind with your departure. Why did you leave?" he asked. No hint of anger, more painful query.

"I thought you didn't want me. And I was scared."

"Of me?"

She shrugged. "Everything. It's been a tough few months since my dad died."

"You're not alone anymore. I will do everything in my

power to keep you safe." He rolled off her and propped himself on his side. "May I?" he asked, raising his hand to hover over her belly.

She nodded.

He palmed her belly, still flat, and yet just this past week the doctor had heard a heartbeat. Which seemed early by her research, but the doctor Theo found her seemed happy with her progress.

In the distance, the sound of sirens broke the night.

"Is there a fire?" she asked.

"Those are police sirens."

"Police? At this time of the night? I wonder what happened."

They found out not long after. The pounding at the door, and the flashing lights illuminating the inside of the curtains, showed the police at the mansion door.

Rory stood in the hall, grim-faced, as the butler opened the door.

Upon being given entry, the steely-eyed man in a uniform stated, "We have an arrest warrant for Rory Lupin Beauchamp."

"I don't understand." She truly didn't. Especially since Rory didn't say anything to refute the charges the police officer accused him of. Attempted murder. Arson.

As handcuffs were placed around Rory's wrists and his rights read, Danita looked to Theo, who stood frail and old in his robe, his white hair tufted atop his head. "Do something."

Theo's lips pressed into thin lines. "I've got a call in to the lawyers, but they won't be able to do anything until the morning. What I'd like to know is, who ratted out my son's presence to the police?"

The police officer began marching Rory out the door. She ran to him, bare feet slapping the floor, her robe cinched tight with her hand.

"Rory!"

He turned to look back at her. "Don't worry, darling. I'll handle this. Stay inside where it's safe. I'll be back in no time."

She flung herself at him for a hard, tingling kiss. Then he was gone. And so was Theo, locked in his office making calls. Danita could only pace and worry. Hours passed, and there was no word. Theo left the house, telling her once more to not worry.

But she did worry. Worried that now that she and Rory had finally decided to give this crazy thing they had a go, she would lose him.

And she'd be alone again.

Please, God, don't take him away from me.

She could only keep repeating that as morning waxed into the noon hour. A lack of appetite and claustrophobia sent her to the garden for a stroll. The walled yard would keep her safe. Theo admitted having it erected to protect his wife's flowers and vegetable garden from deer and other wildlife. Out in the fresh air, she tried to clear her head.

Everything would be fine. Theo would fix this. Rory would come back to her and...Would they really make a life together?

They barely knew each other, but he'd been right

when he said their lives had changed since meeting. Not just because of the baby. He consumed her thoughts. He satisfied her body. And as for her heart? She'd never been one to believe in love at first sight. Heck, she couldn't even claim she loved him from the moment they'd met. He was much too cocky and arrogant for her tastes. However, somewhere along their short journey, she'd seen past his outer shell to the man within. A man who struggled with a past that hurt him. A man with so much passion inside him. At times, he could seem so primal. Almost a beast.

But most of all, he was kind to her. Gentle. Yet fiercely protective.

What more did she want?

I just want him.

And here she was, wandering around outside instead of close to a phone. What if he called? Before she could turn around on the flagstone path, she heard it.

A scrape of a shoe.

She began to whirl to see who joined her. A smelly cloth was slapped over her mouth, and she sank into darkness.

Chapter 18

THE HOURS IN HIS CELL DRAGGED. NOT MUCH TO SEE or do. A toilet with no privacy. A sink that was barely the size of a bowl. A cot with a thin mattress and a gray scratchy woolen blanket. Not exactly what Rory was used to.

It also wasn't a big space. Certainly not wide enough to accommodate any kind of proper pacing. One step, pivot, one step pivot.

Attempts to shake the immovable bars and yelling didn't bring anyone. Glares at the camera watching also went seemingly unnoticed. The worst part of the silence was the wondering what happened.

The guard who brought his breakfast wouldn't say. No one would tell Rory anything. It wasn't until after lunch—a bologna sandwich with mustard and a carton of milk—that someone came to see him.

"Back of the cell," she ordered.

"What's happening?" Rory asked.

"I said, back of the cell." She jerked her finger, pointing.

He shuffled back and leaned against the wall, arms folded over his dull gray, two-piece prison suit. The rubber slippers and gray socks gave it a nice touch.

The metal bars clanged as the officer opened the door to the cell and gestured to Rory. "Let's go."

First things first. "I want to call my lawyer." He'd asked when they were booking him, but they said he'd have to wait until the morning. Which he was pretty sure went against some of his civil rights, but again, not much he could about it until he talked to legal counsel. Known as Connor—who'd been prevented from coming to Canada because some dumbass forgot to renew his passport.

"You can do whatever you like once you leave," said the petite blonde wearing the blue uniform. She'd no sooner slid the door open when she gave him her back as she marched away. "You've been sprung."

About time. He wondered who'd bailed him since he wasn't even given a phone call. He especially worried about Danita. Someone had ratted out his presence.

It should be noted he did have some enemies in the area. All the employees out of work because of his actions. His cousin Bryce, with whom he'd gotten off on the wrong foot.

What if, though, this was part of something more nefarious? What if Kelso had followed Rory?

Is Danita safe? He'd heard nothing since his arrest. Did Elanroux know to keep her safe?

Emerging from the holding cell section, he noted the gray hair of the man dressed in an elegant gray trench coat.

"What are you doing here?" Rory glared at Theo Elanroux.

"Helping."

"The same way you helped my wife hide from me?"

"She requested aid. I gave it to her."

"And neglected to tell me you had her."

"You could have called."

Rory blinked. "I could have called? How the fuck was I supposed to know you even had her?"

"Ahem." The cleared throat turned him to the clerk, who had a manila envelope with his things.

Rory signed for them, grabbed the envelope, and stalked off. Theo followed.

"I didn't know she was your wife when I found her."

"Why were you looking for her?"

"I was asked to go after her by a friend of her father's."

"How did you know where she was?"

"The same friend."

"And when did you know she was my wife?"

Theo's lips pressed.

"You knew when you grabbed her." Stated flatly.

"I did, but she assured me you had no interest in her. And she was frightened. I promised her help. I couldn't say no."

"Hiding her from me."

"It was what she wanted at the time."

Rory glared. "I want to hate you so much right now."

"Understandable."

"Are you the one who ratted me out?" Which he knew made no sense. Why have him arrested then released?

"I had nothing to do with that."

"Someone told the cops I was here."

"Someone did, but I assure you it wasn't me or my staff."

According to him. Rory still wasn't sure of the truth. His wolf had nothing to say on this score. "Why did you come?"

"I thought you might need my help."

"Not from you, I don't." Bitterness colored his words.

"Can't a father try and do the right thing?"

"I have a father."

At that, Theo's lips turned down. "I know. And a fine man, too. A better one than me, apparently, but I'm hoping it's not too late to make amends."

"Bailing me out isn't going to earn you forgiveness."

"Having the charges dropped is a start, though."

"You can't make the charges go away." Arson. Attempted murder. Assault. Rory might have reacted a tad strongly at the discovery he had a second father.

"And yet here you stand, a free man."

Which made no sense. "Who did you bribe?"

"No one."

"Then how? They have evidence." Video footage. Eyewitness accounts. That was, if Bryce Elanroux and his paramour tattled.

"Funny thing about that. It seems they lost their evidence." Theo's lips quirked. "Small towns. Things have a tendency to get misplaced. Oftentimes permanently. No proof, no charges."

The sidewalk outside the police station held pedestrians, walking quickly to their destinations, heads down against the icy wind. "What do you want from me?" Rory asked. Because he doubted Elanroux ever did anything without a motive.

"I want a chance for us to get to know each other."

"What if I don't want to?"

"I understand you're angry right now. What I did to your mother—"

"Angry?" Rory whirled. "This isn't about my mom and the fact you seduced her. Or the fact I now have two daddies. I'm pissed because you kept Danita away from me." Therein lay his real simmering rage.

"I was trying to honor her wishes. She was so hurt when you pushed her away because of the baby."

Rory's lips flattened. "I never pushed. She ran."

"With reason. She overheard you talking to a friend."

She must have been awake in the car when he spoke to Connor. He could have groaned. "I was in shock at the time. I'd just found out about the pregnancy and was trying to process it. Yeah, maybe I didn't immediately do fucking cartwheels, but I've had time since then to realize I don't care who the father is. I just want her back."

"I'm glad to hear that. And assumed you'd patched things up when you did your best to sneak into the house last night."

"You knew I was breaking in?"

Elanroux smiled, and for an uncanny moment, Rory saw himself in the grin. "I've been keeping an eye on you."

For a moment, Rory froze. "If you were, then you knew I was looking for Danita." He also then realized. "You didn't tell me on purpose. You were waiting for me to contact you."

A slight nod.

"And what? Were you going to use her as a bargaining chip to force a relationship?"

"Actually, I was more concerned about my grand-child in her belly."

Rory kept his mouth shut rather than tattle the fact that it might not be his.

Elanroux snorted. "I can read your face, son. Like a younger version of myself. The baby is yours. I even had a test done since I figured you wouldn't believe it."

"Mine." *Fuck me, Danita carries my child!* Now, more than ever, he needed to return to her side. "Tell you what. How about I don't kick your old-man ass for being a manipulative bastard and you take me to Danita now."

"I left her at the house."

Elanroux repeated that several times, rather disbe-lievingly, over the next hour as they searched the place and couldn't find her. The alarm system was disabled. Kendrick knocked unconscious. And Bryce was off with Melanie on a cruise.

"I can't believe you fucking lost her." Rory's accusa-tion wasn't exactly fair. He didn't care.

"I didn't lose her. Someone stole her." They were in the garden, where the smell of cat still lingered. The fucker had marked the lettuce patch.

"You should have had more guards." Dogs. Real ones. The kind that tore the legs off strangers. A cannon, to blow his fucking nuts off. "You knew she was in danger from Kelso."

"He knows who I am." Elanroux puffed his chest. "I didn't think he'd have the balls to come into my territory."

A valid assumption, given Elanroux was on the Chimera Council—the ruling group that kept all shapeshifters from all walks of life in line—as an elder member. Most people accorded them extra respect.

"Yeah, well, think again. Kelso has already crossed a few lines. What's a few more?"

"I noticed. And believe me, this upsets me as much as you."

Doubtful. His bio father didn't have a wolf pacing inside, growling and snapping, ready to draw blood. Rory scrubbed a hand over his face, feeling the rough scrape of his bristles. "I'll have to make some calls. Figure out where she is." Because no way was he letting Kelso put a dirty paw on her.

"No need. I know where he is hiding. She told me about the cabin he kept her prisoner in. I know that cabin, and I'll bet it's where he took her."

Which was how, less than a day later, Rory found himself outside a log cabin in the middle of fucking nowhere surrounded by way too many trees. What the fuck was it with Canada and trees? Everywhere he went, tall ones, fat ones, skinny trunks, fir needles. Give him the wide-open views of the ocean where a man could see for miles. He couldn't wait to go home, but not until he'd found Danita.

And this time, he was in the right place. He could smell not only the man he hunted, but...*my woman.*

Planting his hands on his hips, he opened his mouth and bellowed, "Darling, if you're in there, I'm coming for you!" Perhaps not the most brilliant way of announcing his presence, but he didn't see a doorbell. It worked, though.

Movement at a second-floor window caught his attention. A moment later, a sash shoved open and she appeared, pressing against the bug screen.

The widest smile stretched his lips, especially since she looked unharmed if pale. "Hey, darling, you okay?"

"Are you insane?" she hissed. "Leave before he hears you."

But the whole point of being loud was drawing Kelso's attention. "Like hell I'm leaving. I came to get you." Because, today, Rory got to be a hero—and it felt fucking great.

"I appreciate it, really I do, but it's too dangerous."

"Yeah, those back-country roads are killer on a vehicle's suspension. Good thing I didn't come in the Beemer."

"Rory, don't joke about this. I am talking about real danger. Leave now, please. If you don't, I'm afraid Kelso will kill you."

"He can try."

She growled, and pretty darned well for a human. "Would you stop that? This is not a game. Kelso. Will. Murder. You."

"Do you have so little faith in my abilities, darling?"

He probably shouldn't tease her. He knew her well enough now to realize she'd yet to figure out his furry secret. She wouldn't be in the dark much longer.

"You stupid man. Listen to me," she snapped. "Kelso will tear you apart. He's not normal."

"I know. Don't worry, darling. I've got this covered. And I know I should have done this better, but we don't have time. So, just remember. No matter what you see, I'd never hurt you." With the promise uttered, Rory cupped his hands to his mouth, but rather than bellow, he howled. A long, drawn-out call to action aimed at a cowardly cat.

He ignored Dani's soft and confused "Rory?" to focus on the front door that opened. Out sauntered Kelso, thumbs looped in his pants, a sneer on his face. He wouldn't be smirking for long. Rory planned to rearrange his features.

"Stupid dumb dog. You should have walked away."

"No, you should have walked away. Danita's mine."

"Are you still yapping about that pesky marriage thing? Don't worry. She'll be a widow before long." Kelso beckoned, and men piled onto the porch behind him, the same scruffy crew as before.

"Is that all you got?"

"I'd say we're plenty enough to handle one mangy

cur." Kelso's grin oozed of confidence. Rory couldn't wait to knock it off.

He allowed his own smirk of triumph to appear. "Did you really think I came alone?" Rory whistled and from the woods emerged his backup, an eclectic mix that would have made a certain nature photographer cream his pants.

First emerged a big beast of a moose—cousin Bryce who grumbled about helping Rory, a man he hated, until his mate, Melanie, slugged him in the gut and told him he should be happy to have family.

Next, out stepped a grizzled lynx—Uncle Kieran, Melanie's father, who'd been too late to stop Rory from making a fool of himself the last time he visited his bio father.

If that weren't odd enough, accompanying them were wolves, including Rory's father. A man who'd finally come to his senses and realized that handing Dani over, any woman for that matter, was just fucking wrong.

Lastly, his best friend, Connor—who'd crossed the border illegally—and another buddy of his, Wesley. When they'd heard what happened, they volunteered to help. Theo did, too, but Bryce threatened to put him back in the hospital if he didn't follow the doctor's orders.

"You bastard. You dare think to attack me," Kelso growled.

"You shouldn't have taken what was mine." Rory unbuttoned his shirt.

Kelso tore his right off. "You'll have to fight me if you want her."

"With pleasure."

Kelso jumped down from the porch, his skin rippling with the change. His remaining clothes tearing as his limbs contorted and his body bulked. Fur sprouted from his skin, a light tawny color. Mountain cat claws sprang from his paws as they hit the ground. The feline snarled.

Overhead in the window still, Danita cried out, "Oh my God, I told you he wasn't normal. Run before he eats you. Run!"

Except Rory wasn't about to run. "Remember what I said," he replied. Only now did he wish he'd had an earlier chance to warn Danita about the fact that Kelso wasn't the only one with a furry personality. She was about to find out.

Shifters were just people who had better control of the switch to change their shape into something else. Those who claimed they really were two separate entities? Deluding themselves. His multiple personalities were all about him.

But would Danita recognize that?

Or call him a monster, too?

Come out, come out, wherever you are, he mentally hummed to his wolf. It didn't need any urging. His beast, that primal part of him, rose to the surface, not so much a separate entity as a control over his own biology.

He closed his ears to her sobbed gasp of shock as he finally revealed his wolf.

No need for a mirror. His appearance wouldn't have changed since the last time. Bigger than your average wolf. Tawnier haired, too. No one talked about the two horns on his forehead. Short nubs that gave him a rather fierce appearance.

He stood without moving, head canted toward the window. Danita was gone.

Something he couldn't worry about because the battle was on! Kelso, a mountain cougar, sprang at him with powerful hind legs, his claws slashing. Rory knew to steer clear of those razor-sharp blades. He liked his guts inside his body, thank you. When it came to slashing claws versus his nails meant more for running, Kelso had a clear advantage, which was why Theo had suggested bringing a gun to the fight—*because those mountain cats fight dirty.* But Rory had heard enough old stories to have a certain distaste when it came to firearms. It seemed like cheating somehow. What he didn't have a problem with was a helping hand or—in this case—a helping rack. Bryce—whom he had a hard time thinking of as a nephew because they were of a similar age—came at the cougar with tines lowered. With a snarl to keep Kelso distracted, Rory watched as Bryce charged in and scooped the big kitty. A toss of his head and Kelso flew, hitting the ground hard on his side. So much for the always-land-on-four-feet rule.

Before the cougar could fully recover his wits, Rory tore into him, snarling and snapping, doing his best to avoid those deadly claws. Cats were nimble fuckers, though. A slash across Rory's shoulder left a burning gouge that bled.

Bryce returned to help, taking his turn against Kelso, who spat and hissed and slashed.

When Bryce took a nasty slash to the leg, Rory finally could jump in for a turn. They wrestled, locked in a furry battle of gnashing teeth and flying fur.

Kelso wriggled free and bolted for the house. Made it to the open door and... *Boom!*

A gunshot took off his head.

For a moment, everything paused, a silent moment with eyes trained on Kelso's body. It sank in slow motion to the ground, the neck bubbling hotly. The bloodlust ran hot, as hot as the coppery blood spilled. There were still a few cats standing. Rory helped take care of them before he took a paw toward the cabin. The front door loomed open. The window overhead bare.

He took a second step and paused. He lifted his nose for a sniff. A true inhalation that let him *taste* every scent. Blood, animal musk, and fear. Human fear.

His mate's fear. She wasn't inside the house.

Rory trotted around the side of the building, moving faster as he left the scene of the battle, and her scent became clearer. She'd bolted from the house, and now that he knew that, he ran.

Four paws moving in synchronicity meant he covered the ground more quickly than she. It wasn't long before he heard her panting gasps. The gap between them closed, and she turned to look over her shoulder, eyes wide with fear.

Dammit, don't be scared of me, darling.

She wasn't watching where she ran and tripped over a rock. Her entire body jerked. Her arms flailed. She didn't catch her balance. Toppling forward, she barely managed to get her hands out to break her fall.

He wasn't in time to catch her, even though, moments later, he knelt beside her. As a man.

She cringed from him. "Stay away from me!"

No ignoring the fear in her eyes. Then again, what did he expect? He was covered in blood and naked. Probably not something she'd ever had to deal with before. What he could show her, though, was he meant her no harm. "Don't be scared, darling. It's just me."

"You're one of *them*."

Not the most auspicious inflection. "I'm a Lycan."

"Which is a werewolf."

"Yes."

"Like Kelso."

"Nothing like that asshole," he said most vehemently. The sharp bite of his words had her flinching. He softened them. "I might be a shapeshifter, but you have to believe me when I say I'd never hurt you."

"But I saw you. Fighting."

"To save you. Because you and I both know Kelso wasn't about to hand you over."

"I know. It's why I shot him."

He'd wondered when the shot came from the house. The courage it must have taken to step up and do what had to be done. "He can't ever hurt you again."

"Can't he? When the police find out what I did—"

"They won't find out. There's a reason you were surprised we really existed, and that's because we know how to wipe our tracks. Which means don't worry about Kelso. No one will ever know what happened."

"Is that what happened to my dad? Did Kelso kill him?"

An intriguing question. "We will have to look for the answer. I'm just happy you and the baby are safe. My baby."

"Yours..." Her face blanched. "Will the baby be—"

"Special? Possibly. Although it remains to be seen whether that will be moose or wolf."

"Moose?" she squeaked.

"Blame my paternal line for that."

She licked her lips before asking, "That was Theo outside?"

"No, my nephew Bryce. Which makes you that moose's aunt."

She closed her eyes. "This is insane."

"You'll get used to it."

"What if I don't want to?"

"You will because you love me." He lifted her in his arms.

"Says who?"

"Says me. The man who loves you, too."

Her nose wrinkled. "You do?"

"More than you can imagine."

And he did his best to show her. Making love to her in the master bedroom of the cabin, after stripping all the beds and burning the linen. The house stunk of cat. But he'd not wanted to rush back with the others, especially when she'd murmured against his neck, "The cabin has hot water."

Which is how they found themselves, skin to skin, their bodies flushed and throbbing, his cock balls deep in her. Their foreheads were touching as they rocked in rhythm, and the only thing he could think was, *Damn, this is the life.*

"I love you," he gasped as he came.

"I love you," she murmured as she fell asleep in his arms.

Rory woke to a gun pointed at his forehead, the scent of angry cat, and a lowly growled, "How dare you defile my baby girl!"

Epilogue

Dani woke to her father's voice threatening. *Am I dreaming?* She quickly blinked away her confusion as she noticed the situation was very real. Her father aimed a gun at Rory, and looked ready to use it. "Daddy, don't kill him!"

"Don't get involved, pumpkin. And look away. Daddy's gonna take care of this problem."

"There's no problem. Put that gun away."

"I kind of like where it is." The barrel pressed, dimpling Rory's skin, and Dani snapped.

"You stop that right now and start explaining how come you're here. I thought you were dead."

"I'm not that easy to kill."

Now where had she heard that before?

"A pleasure to, um, meet you, sir," Rory tried to say politely, extending his hand.

"Not for you it isn't." Her father's golden eyes glared at her husband.

"Where have you been?" Dani asked. "I've been worried sick. And this guy called Kelso—"

"Kelso? Where is that mangy bastard? I'm going to tear off his head and shove it up his ass."

"I shot him," she said, rather pertly. She'd gotten over the first shock of it. Shooting someone wasn't easy. But she'd already come to the realization she'd done the world a favor. The healing could begin.

"You had to kill a man?" The gun pressed harder as Daddy snarled, "You didn't protect my girl!"

"He was protecting me fine. Stop that. He's not the one who abandoned me."

Familiar tawny eyes swung her way. "I didn't abandon you, pumpkin. I was detained."

"For months."

"Not on purpose. And during the short period I was gone, according to the report I was handed, you managed to get kidnapped numerous times. What the fuck, Dani?"

"Don't raise your voice to her," Rory intervened.

"Does the defiler truly think he should be talking?" Her father's gaze swung hotly back to Rory. "Any last words before I kill you?"

"Daddy, no. You can't kill him. You've got it all wrong. Rory saved me."

"From what? Because, from where I'm standing, it looks like he didn't save you from his depraved actions."

Depraved? Now she did snicker. "Rory didn't do anything I didn't want."

This caused the gun to lift and her father to slap

hands over his ears, exclaiming, "I don't want to hear this."

She clutched at the sheet and knelt on the bed. "Daddy. Stop being silly. It's not what you think. He's my husband."

"Husband?" Her father's eyes swung to Rory and narrowed. "You married her? Why?"

"It was actually an accident. We were drunk in Vegas, but—" The rest of her words never emerged because her daddy bellowed, "Filthy dog!" And then... Daddy was a lion.

She gaped.

Rory sighed. "Ah, fuck. I guess this explains why Kelso wanted you."

"What are you talking about?" she said, wincing when her father—a giant kitty—roared and paced by the bed.

"I think a whole lot just became clear. Kelso killed your daddy to take over his position in the pride."

"What does pride have to do with it?"

"Not that kind of pride. I'm talking pride as in a group of lions. And other shapeshifting cats. Your daddy is the lion king, and as his daughter, you were the binding tie Kelso needed to get them to fall into place."

"But I'm not a lion." The very idea of being one was too hard to even grasp. Seeing the giant kitty—*my daddy*—pacing alongside the bed didn't help. How could she not have known? *What does that make me?*

"You probably carry the gene."

"I'm a freak."

The cat roared.

She snapped back. "Don't you dare. This is pretty big news to drop on me."

"It's not easy to explain."

"You think?" she said with exaggeration. "I just don't understand how I didn't know. Did my mother know? Were you ever going to tell me?"

Her father chuffed.

Rory translated. "My guess is he would have told you if you showed signs of changing. My guess is your mother was human, and when your father realized you didn't carry the gene, he kept you away from the pride and the politics for safety reasons."

"So I wouldn't be used as a pawn. But Kelso found out."

Another roar.

"Oh, stop that. He's dead." Said with some pride. She'd not needed anyone to rescue her, after all. But she appreciated Rory had tried.

She quickly averted her eyes as her lion daddy became just plain daddy again—minus clothes. "Daddy!"

"Don't freak out, baby girl. I'm grabbing some pants."

"I'll freak out if I want to," she huffed. "I've had a lot happen lately."

"Because of the fucker Kelso. I can't believe that two-timing bastard tried to kill me."

"He seemed very sure you were dead."

"More like incapacitated in a jungle and held captive for a while by a tribe of indigenes who worshipped me."

She blinked.

"I'll explain after I deal with this so-called husband of yours," grumbled her father.

To which she replied, "Don't you dare kill my baby's daddy!"

"No, please don't tell me I'm related to dogs."

Whereupon Rory held out his hand and said, "Nice to finally meet the elusive lion king."

The next few hours, after everyone found clothes, they exchanged stories while raiding the kitchen for food. Gregory's kitchen, because it turned out Kelso had brought Danita to her own father's house.

"I can't believe you had another place to live," she grumbled, still trying to absorb all the many secrets and lies peppering her life.

Daddy didn't look the least chagrinned. "Don't get all pissy. I didn't spend much time here. But I needed a place to meet with pride members."

Pride members as in lions.

Danita eventually did wrap her head around it. Just like she learned that were-shifters did things a little differently. For one, Daddy officially presented his daughter to the pride and then warned everyone that to harm her would result in death. To which Rory added a ditto. Cute and embarrassing all at once.

Her father and her new father-in-law—the wolf one, not the moose one—also announced their new alliance. Dogs and cats working together, which apparently was a huge, big deal. All she noted was it involved lots of drinking, roaring, and howling, and pregnant bellies popping up in the months after. Rory was particularly pleased when he got his two fathers to agree on a joint project between their companies that involved doing something sweet and salty. Which she didn't crave at all. But pasta? Dani couldn't get enough.

Just like she couldn't get enough of Rory. True to his word, and despite Daddy's objections, he took her home to the seashore, where married life agreed with them both.

They'd been living and loving for months now, and according to the doctor—a shifter one who would keep their special secret—any day the baby was going to come. The shorter gestation an almost sure sign she was going to have a shifter baby.

But she wasn't scared. Not anymore. She'd had months to meet the people in her father's pride and Rory's wolf pack. People just like her, but who had a super-duper cool power. She chose to see them as hidden superheroes rather than monsters. As for Kelso? He was just a supervillain, and in the end, the natural order had prevailed. The good guys won.

Life was epic. She not only still had her daddy, she had a wonderful new life on the beach, and everyone was carefully getting along.

"You're up early." Rory's arms slid around her from behind, cupping her belly as he nuzzled her hair.

She stared from the balcony at the ocean, the soothing roll and tumble of waves one of her favorite things to watch.

A happy sigh echoed from her. "I love you." The words slipped from her lips, truer now than ever.

Being a man, raised in the spirit of competitiveness, he, of course, had to reply, "I love you more."

For some reason, she found this funny. She laughed so hard her water broke—on his feet.

By the next morning, their family had grown with the addition of Jasmyn Helena Beauchamp, their special Vegas baby.

THE END

Classic romance... with a furry twist!

Did you enjoy this Howls Romance story?

If YES, check out the other books in the Howls Romance line by

heading over to : HowlsRomance.com

OR CHECK OUT MORE EVE BOOKS AT
EVELANGLAIS.COM